MW00989507

"SOUL-SI

"*Soul Sister* is a moving and psyche-wrenching success. . . . An intensely personal account of our worst American tragedy . . . recorded with a kind of appalled humanity."

"Provocative and eye-opening."

"I am not a man who cries, but I was moved to cry by what Grace Halsell wrote. . . . Her book is beautiful."

"EXTRAORDINARY. . . . A STARTLING ACCOUNT."

SOUL SISTER

GRACE HALSELL

Crossroads International Publishing
Washington, D.C.

Crossroads International Publishing
P.O. Box 42058
Washington, D.C. 20015

http://members.aol.com/CRoadsInt
E-mail: CRoadsInt@aol.com

Cover Design:
DESKTOP MIRACLES
Stowe, VT

Preface

October, 1999

In the late 1960s, I was working as a staff writer in the White House for President Johnson. Walking the corridors of power, I felt myself very lucky: I had a high-prestige, high-paying job.

One day I overheard Zephyr Wright, LBJ's favorite cook and the only black woman working in the White House, telling of her travail driving to and from Texas. Once, when Johnson was a senator, he asked her to take two dogs along. "You have *no idea,*" she told him, "what it is like for a Negro to try to get a decent motel room—and you are asking me to take two dogs?"

Hearing that story, I wondered: what was it like to live as a Negro woman?

Leaving my White House job, I consulted with leading dermatologists at Yale and Howard universities. They told me about a medication, which, taken in conjunction with exposure of my body to intense tropical sun, would darken my skin. Lying on a Caribbean island, I noticed, day by day, a dramatic change in my color. One day I looked in a mirror and saw a "black" woman looking back at me.

After living in Harlem, I later went to Mississippi. I found all the facilities and institutions totally segregated. I rode buses, stayed in the homes of black families—who knew I was white passing as black—and who helped me find jobs. Often I stood on a Jackson, Mississippi street corner, waiting for a white housewife, who, through an agency, had hired me for the day. I found no job opportunities other than working as a maid. And the most I could make was $5 a day.

Now, after more than three decades, what has changed? What progress have we made in overcoming the legacy of slavery? I feel assured that if now I returned to re-live my *Soul Sister* experiences, I would not be arrested, as I was back in the late 1960s, for stepping from a segregated black section of a bus station into a more commodious white section—asking to use a telephone.

The wooden walls segregating blacks have been removed. With darkened skin, I would be able to sit in "white" restaurants, stay in "white" hotels, drink from fountains formerly designated for "whites only."

And I know that today, with darkened skin, were I to walk into a white church, the Christians of that church would not—as they did back then—call the police and have me arrested.

Today, on film clips, we see and hear the voices calling for change: we hear Martin Luther King and his "dream" and we remember Rosa Parks, who refused to give up her seat on a segregated bus, and we buy commemorative stamps of Malcolm X, who moved from endorsing exclusive black and white societies to a "world" where we live as brothers and sisters. And we remember the leadership of Lyndon Johnson, who, reared in a southern atmosphere of racism and discrimination, moved beyond his heritage and prejudices to accomplish more for blacks and equal rights than any of our Presidents with the exception of Lincoln.

Based largely on the changes, that came as an aftermath of the struggles in the 1960s, African-Americans have made significant economic and political progress in the past 30 years.

The Klu Klux Klan no longer operates with impunity, but we have a new generation of "white supremacists" fostering racial hatred and using affirmative action as their main target.

When, in a 1965 Howard University commencement speech, President Johnson first defined affirmative action, he made no reference to racial preferences or quotas. He defined affirmative action as having a level playing field, as providing minorities with an "equal opportunity" in education and employment.

The enemies of civil rights have organized a nationwide effort against an affirmative action, redefined to mean racial preferences and quotas.

In many parts of the country, including Washington, D.C., there is less mixing among whites and blacks socially today than in the 1960s, when top government officials and popular hostesses openly and enthusiastically embraced "integration" with a certitude they were prescient and right.

While much has changed politically and economically for blacks, not much has advanced in social terms of integration. As we move into a new century, the tragedy and severity of our racial problems remain.

— Grace Halsell

THIS IS FOR MY MOTHER

*She knows suffering can bring
understanding; that understanding
frees one to love—without limits.*

.

CONTENTS

SOUL SISTER

GRACE HALSELL

Crossroads International Publishing
Washington, D.C.

Prologue

January, 1969

NIGHT AFTER NIGHT I have had this dream—it is a busy street in mid-Manhattan and strong men in steel hats drill their power tools into the earth to lay more ducts and more sewers to create a greater New York. Buses and taxis screech and whirl; the subway grinds and hurtles; and thousands of people scurry, guided by lights, bells, signals: "Follow the green arrow," "Follow the red arrow." I am one of the mass of men, moving relentlessly, ceaselessly. And I pass a manhole and see the face of a child, a doll's face, large, white, round; and doll's eyes that look but see nothing. And I scream, "It is a child!" I reach but realize the doll-child is beyond my grasp, and the body floats past and returns in a liquid casing, appearing caught up in some underground eddy.

The people run faster, and I scream "Help! Police!", and three policemen, strong and rough, bear down on me, heedless of the child and of my pleas for the child. They arrest me. I shriek, plead with them but I am helpless, and they carry me away to their jail. . . .

This recurring nightmare was a psychological mirror of the helplessness and terror I had experienced as a woman turned black by medication and the sun, who had gone to live and

3

work in Harlem and the deep South. The shock I suffered had left my spirit maimed and my mind in turmoil.

From Jackson I flew to Memphis to make a connection home. I stood in some nether world for four hours in the airport, my mind grappling with the physical, mental, and spiritual barriers to re-entering the white world. My stomach churned with the tension it contained. It is my first line of defense against all griefs and fears; others get headaches, sophisticated twinges in the neck and twitches here and ticks there, but my belly is bell-wether and alarm and it shouts and scuffles and flips, and I am the referee.

At midnight, I put the key into my Washington apartment door, open it two inches and I come apart, breaking into tears I can't control. Inside—all that comfort, all those luxuries! I have been frightened and alone, and I must stand still on the outside looking in, to *exist* for a moment longer outside that door as a black woman, as a menial, beyond expectations or hope. Then I moved my bag inside and I went to my bed and cried without shame. My tears gushed from sources of which I myself was not aware and they gave no sounds.

Around me were all my shelves of books, my pictures on the walls, my *things*. I groped for reality and I finally felt secure and *grateful*. God! a gratitude to be alive. But I wanted to see no one, for my adjustment was acutely personal and I dared not face the possible fact that I was in a trauma and had a healing period to undergo, that I needed time. I stayed in my apartment for days, losing track of time and knowing I could not yet leave this protective cell, womblike, warm, undemanding.

After two weeks, Roscoe Dixon, the black maintenance man and my friend, came by with a cake his wife Dorothy had baked. "Aren't you ever goin' turn on the music?" he asked, and without waiting flipped on my favorite station, one with *latino* music. He urged my getting out for "some fresh air," and I went across the street to Hella's beauty shop. Mr. Henry, who has frequently given me a set, now washed my raven hair without recognizing me. Putting in the curlers, he spoke to me as he would a dour stranger: "Don't you ever smile?" he asked.

Later I told Roscoe, "That ole whitey expected me to be *smiling* at him. I'm not wasting my smiles on him!"

I turned my phone off so that all calls would go to the switchboard downstairs. "Aren't you going to see any of your friends?" Roscoe asked. "Not any *white* people," I told him.

So I passed unnatural days, not feeling black or white, only a recluse.

One day I went to the Watergate Health Club. Seeing me, the director reacted as if he had seen a ghost. "What have you done to yourself?" he asked, obviously grieved. "I must tell you you look at least ten years older. And if you tell me you've been in prison, and brutally beaten . . . whatever horrible tale you tell me, I can believe you. Tell me," he insisted, *"what happened to you!"*

I said it would take time to explain.

Part I

THE
BEGINNING

The Beginning

THE BEGINNING is sometimes as simple and undramatic as an exchange of pleasantries. I attended a Plans for Progress reception, mingling in the State Department diplomatic rooms with about two thousand big business VIPs who had "pledged" to treat Negro employees as fairly as whites. Afterward I ate dinner with a couple of the visiting executives.

"What caused you to become *personally* interested?" I asked a Bell Helicopter vice-president.

"When I read *Black Like Me*," he replied.

The title meant nothing to me. Perhaps I was in Turkey, Korea, or Arabia when the book came out. And I hadn't heard of the author, John Howard Griffin, although we came from the same home town, Fort Worth, Texas. The next day I bought *Black Like Me* and plunged into it, discovering that Griffin talked to me like an inner voice, calm, suggestive. "I could do that . . . I could be black."

At lunch, two male associates, a woman friend and I (we all worked at the White House) were talking about *the* problem facing the country.

"If anyone is willing to work . . . !" Mary began, her bias

9

etched in grimly set lips, saying I-was-born-poor, I-worked-hard, I-made-it.

Since Mary and I are both from Texas, I wondered aloud: "What difficulties you and I might have had, born poor, Southern, and *black*, to have gotten such good jobs in the White House."

Mary said, defensively, "I'd probably be making more money!" But we both knew there were black cleaning women making as little as two hundred dollars a month—and no black women earning anything like our salaries.

"We could blacken our faces, travel by car to Texas—and see how we'd be treated, checking into motel rooms, eating in restaurants," I suggested. I had heard LBJ's cook, Zephyr Wright, telling of her travail driving to and from Texas, and once when Mr. Johnson, then a senator, asked her to take two dogs along, she made it plain that being black—and traveling through the South—provided more than enough difficulties, without adding the dogs!

February, 1968

THE SEED IS PLANTED, it grows. I have not reasoned it there nor nourished it logically. Imagination, feeling, cause it to grow. (And what makes men different could be feeling rather than reason.) I had only to imagine myself black and then, for the first time, I saw myself *white!* This puzzled, unsettled me. Each craves to affirm himself, if only in appearance, and yet this struggle to singularize is a thousand times more terrible than the struggle for life. Troubled, I reached back in time, into the recesses of memory and experience.

I was born and grew up in Texas, a descendant of slave-holders and Civil War veterans. But color was not a conscious fact in my early years. I never regarded Negroes as a part of my society. I had no particular feelings about them, one way or another. They were simply a part of the landscape.

Since that time I have traveled around the world as a free-lance newspaper reporter and have had an opportunity to observe all races. I have come to know them, to love and—sometimes—hate them as autonomous human beings, sovereign, proud, timid, submissive, craven, and brave, yet with a singular identity.

Most white people still think of Negroes as somehow different and apart. They see their skin and nothing else. The depths of sensitivity, attitudes, abilities, emotions escape this superficial, subliminal view. I wanted to write a story revealing how much alike we all are. And I wanted to do it directly, from the most personal experience, so that I could actually feel the common-ality and communicate it to others.

I asked myself: how could I be sure I understood this feeling unless I passed as a Negro in the South—and in Harlem—and subjected myself to the same problems that a Negro woman must cope with day in and day out?

After all, *Black Like Me* was written by a man, and since Griffin infiltrated the black community (1959) times for Negroes in general have changed. The right to sit anywhere in a bus, to be served a hamburger at a dime-store counter, to choose your own seat in a movie theater—most Negroes have realized these demands, but they are only too agonizingly con-scious that they are still being treated as second-class citizens. I wondered if it were possible for a white woman to expose herself to that mind-deadening malady of second-class citizenship and report its effects.

It seemed to me I was in a good position to notice all the fetters binding my darker sisters. No white (first-class) citizen could have enjoyed more freedom of movement than I have had.

Obviously, if my parents had been black, even though I had been born with the same talents that I, a white child, was born with, chances would have been strongly against my succeeding as a free-lance journalist who wound up working as a Presidential aide in the White House.

Knowing that each man is unique, irreplaceable, I wanted to find a personal answer to the question of precisely how whites treat a "Mary Doe," an individual with training and background, identical with mine, even using my own name. I would be black in their eyes but the same person I had always been.

March, 1968

I HAVE NO IDEA how old Roscoe Dixon might be. "They never show their age," as white people say about black people. Dixon worked twenty years as a cook at Freedmen's Hospital, then came to work as a cleanup man at the Calvert House apartment building in which I live. And soon after we met, he began bringing me roses, fresh corn on the cob, and fresh black-eyed peas from his garden. He told me about himself, his wife, Dorothy, "a good woman," their grown children and ten grandchildren.

Once when Roscoe was in my apartment he picked up a paperback of *Black Like Me*. "Take it . . . on loan," I suggested. This morning he brought it back.

"Man," he began. "What he went through. . . ." And he recalled graphically the details of the Southern bus driver not permitting Griffin to get off the bus to go to the rest room, of the Negro who picked him up on the lonely dark highway and shared his "nothingness" with Griffin, and of Griffin sleeping on a hard floor and walking out into the night, "crying like a baby."

"Dixon," I asked, standing in the luxury of my wall-to-wall carpeting, "do you think I could do what Griffin did?"

"Unh-unh," he replied, in a vigorous, head-shaking negative. He didn't think there was "a man alive" could do what Griffin did, "taking all that shame." I suggested that millions of black men and women did it every day. "But," he pointed out, "that's different—when you're *born* black, you get prepared for the shame."

Dixon didn't realize it, but his remarks only deepened my determination. Was this determination founded on an unconscious guilt feeling? Did it spring from my curiosity as a trained reporter who wants to find out the true facts at first hand? Why was I really going to do it? My emotions answered: I need this experience. I have been on the outside looking in. I have smelled the colored people's collard greens and their living-up-close-together smells. I am now going to knock on their doors and say, black people let me in there with you!

And if they open the door for me, what must I "give up"— leave on the outside, as it were? It's not that I want pain but that one has discomfort when he gives up comfort. It's not that I want to rip up my carpeting and go live on bare floors, but that one chooses between truth and repose, and choosing means a *giving up*.

My history of "giving up" began when I left home-based security and went off to make my way around the world. When I returned in 1953 after years of writing home-town dispatches for a number of Southwestern daily newspapers from an assortment of world capitals, I went to work for an oil company, as public relations director. "You can be anything you want in this company," the president said. By 1955, I was making $1,000 a month and enjoying such fringe benefits as the use of company planes. But the money and the perquisites left me dissatisfied and unfulfilled. I felt shackled. There had to be a larger meaning to my life. I thought often of the Orient as a possible source of self-discovery. Abruptly in 1956, "I'm leaving—for Japan," I told the president.

"I think you're making a mistake," he said. No one in this world could have absolute freedom, he told me, but those with money in their pockets could approach it. He urged me to stay where I was. I set off anyway.

Japan, Korea, Hong Kong, Arabia, Greece, Turkey—I kept writing my way around and around. South America. I went there in 1959 with little money, not knowing a word of Spanish. And stayed three years. And to Washington, and got a job as a reporter. In 1965 President Johnson saw me in the pack of regulars trailing him on one of his fabled walks around the south lawn of the White House. "Come over here, you are the prettiest thing I ever saw!" The next week he called me, and hired me as a staff writer. And I stayed three years.

Now, with a prestige position, I could play status quo, bank on social security, and visualize retirement benefits; in short, get *through* the rest of my life without *living* it. But I decided to risk insecurity. And experience what others with greater insecurity must bear, and write of these experiences as one imprisoned by a black skin, trying to register the ineffable despair.

April 3, 1968

"I WANT TO KNOW YOU," I wrote John Howard Griffin. He would be in Baltimore to make a speech; I wrote suggesting that I pick him up in Baltimore and that we drive back to Washington, where he could get a plane for his next stop. We arranged to meet at a Howard Johnson coffee shop. He was wearing colored glasses, and I presumed that since his period of blindness (the result of injuries received in World War II), his eyes are still sensitive to glare or light, although his sight has been restored.

He told me that in recent weeks he had undergone major surgery because of a rare condition—certain bones were disappearing and as one bone began to disintegrate the doctors rushed and replaced it with steel. "You are no longer a man," one surgeon kidded him, "but a work of art!" We were intuitively close and understanding, like friends who have known each other in trust and affection all their lives.

Driving back to Washington we discussed a variety of subjects, never touching on the reason why I had driven to Baltimore to meet him. Nor did he once voice any curiosity. I had determined not to speak on the subject—unless questioned—until much later in the evening.

Leaving him at the Shoreham Hotel, across the street from my apartment, I dashed to the supermarket and bought lamb chops. He came over to eat with me, and we sat around talking.

At length, I handed him a memo setting forth what I proposed to do. He read it quietly, and with great feeling responded immediately: *"Oh, yes, you have to do it."*

Griffin said he had always wished that a woman could do what he had done, because there were so many feelings that black women must have—watching their beloved children grow up to be despised by some simply because of the color of their skin—and that he could never penetrate the feelings of a woman, of a mother, as I might be able to do. He said that since he had written *Black Like Me* many women had come to him with the idea that they might try what he did. "But I discouraged every one, because—until you—I never met anyone I thought could do it."

April 4, 1968

I FLEW TO TEXAS on the President's plane, Air Force One. A White House limousine called for me at my apartment to take me to Andrews Air Force Base in nearby Maryland. I was deeply stirred by my long evening with Griffin, and more determined than ever to execute my plan. It was paradoxical, and a little ridiculous, that I could think of a project so far removed from the sense of status, of dignity, of security—yes, of power—of my White House position. Inside the long, luxurious blue-and-white jet, Dean Rusk played bridge all the way to Austin. Lynda Bird, kibitzing, chatted about Chuck Robb, her Marine Corps husband, in Vietnam. My mind was partially turned to Griffin, who also would be returning to Texas, by a different route.

That evening I walked into mother's home and she said, "Martin Luther King has been shot!" My first reaction was,

"It's all hopeless. We will fail as a people and a nation." Then I gradually realized that each of us must try to fulfill his dream of one America and I remember fortifying myself with the thought that one can kill a person but not an idea.

I gave a talk at the college in Denton, to some girl journalism students. I talked about free-lancing ("that's writing mostly for free") and related that my sister Margaret (in the audience) had once commented, "We know God takes care of you, but why do you make it so hard on Him?"

Margaret had driven me to Denton. Afterward, she turned her car on the highway that runs due south, and her headlights revealed the straight ribbon of road, stretching out before us like an eternity. We seemed enveloped in the warm, lonely darkness that invited us to leave off talk of clothes, furniture, society, politics, and to unveil the human heart. Yes, I should have liked to have opened my heart to Margaret. Yes, I should like to tell all my family. I needed their support and surely they would be hurt when they learned I had denied them the right of helping me.

Griffin, in our first meeting, had asked: "Have you told your family?"

"No, not yet . . . I was wondering . . . I was going to ask what you might advise. . . ."

"You can tell them when it's over."

"I'm sure my sister would be for this plan," I ventured.

"If you tell one, then the others will be more hurt that you did not tell them also." Yes, I feel this to be true. If there is anyone I want to tell more than the rest it is Mother. I feel my obligation to her, because she has assumed her role to the fullest: to live her life in her children. I know that she "feels" this development, that she all but knows what I am about to do, without knowing it.

Mother, if I should tell you what I will do, I would like also to say I do it because of you. You caused me to have these feelings, to want something more than comfort out of life. I learned at your knee that the life without contemplation is a kind of death. I learned from you to think of giving, not of getting. I learned from you to think of comforting, not of being comforted.

And what I want to do is so simple, Mother. To let the word become the deed; to put others first; to say that after all is said and done, what is important is to live with love for others.

April 8, 1968

To JOHN HOWARD GRIFFIN's home for dinner, where I met his wife, children, and Charles Rector, a young Negro painter who came out of the slums of St. Louis, and has been a narcotics addict. The Griffin's youngest child, Mandy, ran to Charles's arms. "Come, Sweetness!" he had called, and he lifted her in a fast, swinging motion, then held her close to his face, she looking at him worshipfully.

I felt myself buoyed upward, too, propelled by an emotional truth, and I thought: that love is our love, that child might be his child, my child, our child. I felt lifted beyond, above myself, suspended—as if we were all bound in a blessedness that, for the moment, embraced love and tolerance and truth. In the center of that circle sat Griffin, saintly and benign, a wellspring of faith and love that radiated in the eyes of the *black* painter and Mandy, the glowing *blonde* child, a universal love that

denies color and race, an innocence that surmounts the bound-
aries and the barriers of a caste-minded society.

I told a Texas businessman, an acquaintance of long standing, about the strong impact that Mandy and the black painter
had on me. "Do you want to marry him?" the white man asked.
I was momentarily stunned. His question shook me because
with the question came a realization that I had never for a
moment considered the physical aspects of the painter, or
imagined a physical relationship, even as I conceived that the
child could be ours, the product of black and white loins, his
and mine.

As I pondered his question, I remembered what I had heard:
that many white men are convinced that if a white woman talks
to a black man or even looks at a black man she must be
sexually attracted to him.

"But why would you think of that?" I asked finally. "It
never entered my mind! I 'love' him for himself, and it wouldn't
matter to me if he were man, woman, or child."

April 17, 1968

I DROVE TO VIRGINIA to meet Sarah Patton Boyle, who lives alone
in a small apartment. In her *Desegregated Heart*, she writes of
being a well-bred, gentile, Southern white who took on the
mass of Negro people to love, and of her disillusionment in
learning that for all of her ideals, her aspirations, and fondest
hopes she attained little satisfaction or spiritual sustenance.

Her experience was somewhat similar to one that I had in Korea. My heart had bled for the mass of Koreans. Later I saw that I could not love "a people" out of my egotistical "pity" for their poverty or their plight. But I have never felt that I loved the mass of black people, or the mass of white people, nor have I ever been an activist, a do-gooder. And I am *not* my brother's keeper.

Since I chanced to think how would I be treated, if I were black, I have begun to change. I see fat, rich women in the Watergate Health Club who pay hundreds of dollars to lose one pound, contrasted vividly with Rebecca, the black cleanup woman, who holds down two jobs, gets her exercise naturally, and probably has the best figure in the spa.

I began to see how hard most black women like Rebecca must work. And then I began to fear: can I stand up to that kind of pace? How many hours will I have to work? If I used my status as a white and became a cash-stand operator or a telephone operator I'd be a slow learner. I have learned most everything in life slowly, but because I functioned as a white, others have great patience with me. My slow speech, my slow motions are considered quite charming. But as a black girl will I be considered "just a little dumb"?

I wrote a letter to Dr. Robert Stolar, a Washington skin specialist, who *Esquire* magazine said had turned many blacks white. The *Esquire* article stated, "It is easier for a white man to make himself black than for a black man to make himself white," but I don't believe the writer tried either transition himself.

April 18, 1968

CALLED DR. STOLAR's office, made an appointment.

April 19, 1968

WENT TO SEE DR. STOLAR at 2:30. Waited in his office an hour, getting nervous all the while. I'm so impatient of persons who keep me waiting. I remind myself that as a black woman I will need a lot more patience than I now possess. When I finally see Dr. Stolar I talk only briefly about the medicine to turn white skin black, telling him I will come back again, soon.

May, 1968

NOT TO KNOW what one wants, said Santayana, is a simple kind of abdication.

I have wanted three things in my life, and I have been willful. I wanted to marry Clay, and I did. I wanted to travel overseas and around the world, and it meant giving up marriage. I did that too. And now being black has become an all-consuming objective.

Probably at each of these stages if I had been asked, "And why?" I could not have stated the reasons with any clarity or logic. In each case, I yielded to my own concepts of purpose and reason for being, conditioned by emotion and a sense of rightness. If there was a lapse of good judgment, there was nonetheless a definite commitment that was total. And now, I wonder: Can I be logical and reasonable, *as well as willful?*

My life has been more an adventure than a discipline, and yet I feel I've inadvertently been preparing for years for what I will do now. And I want *to learn, not to teach*. This too will be an adventure. Yet, also, I hope to feel the apertures of my heart stretched. Yes, I still might grow, share, learn.

Only in the moment one is ready to give it up can he really appreciate what he loves. Only in this moment have I learned to love my present home. Now in these moments each shelf of my apartment that I touch is touched with love. Here is my castle, my refuge, my shelter. My quiet haven. It is the rock on which I stand. Here are all the possessions that I have, and the shelves all over the place, the shelves with books. The place smells of my smells, the mirrors reflect all of my longing—these years—to have the home that is now my home. And what is the meaning of going out to live as a black woman if I do not give up this place which I now love, to which I now cling? Giving it up means some kind of total break with my past life.

But merely to move myself *physically* from one apartment to another would mean nothing; the journey will have to be within. And how does one journey away from untruths, the old myths that are not spoken but are rather a part of the atmosphere and accepted like the sunlight and the earth beneath you? Whites are superior. Blacks are *different*. They are sometimes quite clever, always have "rhythm," and usually act happy-go-lucky.

I believed in Santa Claus when I was a child and sometime, as time is measured, after I learned or came to know that no man slid down the chimney to leave toys, I came to know that the white man is not superior. Yet even now hidden in an old chest, perhaps in my mother's Texas home, I might come across a relic of the olden days, the stocking I had hung back in the days when I believed in Santa Claus. . . . And there would be other buried relics of which I am not now aware.

Since making the decision to live awhile as a black woman I have been happier. I had not realized this except that in all the letters from family and my best girl friend, Jo, I have read the comments, "You seem so happy!" "Everything seems to be going so well with you!" "You seem to have all of your ducks in a row." And I know that what is making me happy is the idea of giving up comfort and luxury.

At a cocktail party in my apartment, several friends were discussing the possibility, as one solution to the "black problem," of dividing the United States into two countries, one for the whites and the other for the blacks. The idea being of course to "give" the blacks such states as Mississippi and Alabama, rather than Michigan and Illinois.

The words and sentences flowed, but through the chatter I heard the phrase, "Give 'em a blanket and a hundred pounds of beef a month."

One man said, "Many Negroes would go for that."

"How can the whites always assume they know what Negroes would like?"

"Oh," he insisted, "it would be *very* popular with the Negroes."

So, in his brand of *apartheid*, he'd put the blacks in a compound and say stay there, as we did with the few remaining Indians.

May 24, 1968

IN THE FIVE MONTHS that I have imagined being black, I have seen myself as *black and ugly*, in lace-up working shoes and a dark, cheap cotton dress that hangs on my body like a flour sack. And why? Because I am still a member of *the club*, brainwashed to believe that white ladies and pink ladies are naturally more attractive than caramel and chocolate ones. Yes, I have hated to think of myself as *dark* and I have recalled that Elizabeth Arden once told me, "Light hair around the face softens a woman's features. A woman over thirty should never dye her hair black. This will harden her features."

Clarence Robinson, a black man, and I walked along the Potomac, and I heard myself spilling over with talk, the way I'd talked when I was a teen-ager and walked with friends along other rivers, the Hudson in New York, and later the Seine in Paris, the Danube in Vienna, the Rhine in Germany. In those times, life seemed only to have begun, and we spent hours talking of what we wanted in life and of all those marvelous dreams of the young and hopeful.

"Were you ever married?" Robinson asked. Yes, I replied, and then I wanted to wrap up my life for him and for myself in a few brief sentences, and to do so by capturing those forces or persons outside my life that influenced me.

I told him I had been strongly influenced by my father, who, when I was born, was the age at which we picture Socrates, and who always had urged me to go, seek, knock; if I did so, doors would be opened, he said. "Why," he had even told me, "you might become Governor!" And to Texans that was more than being President. He said there were no limits for the mind. And he was interested in the Great Questions: what are you here for? where are you going? He never said "don't" to me, but rather urged the positive: go and live life as an adventure.

Ironically, then I met and married Clay, who, like a police-man, warned me to stay away from the unfamiliar. "Baby girl, *be careful*," he always told me.

To sum up Clay's life, as I said to the black man: "He lived in a world that was all black and white. . . ." The statement gave me pause because it could be misinterpreted. I meant that Clay lived in a world with no gray in it. His was a world that was all white (good) and all black (bad, wrong, evil).

Now, when I am black will I want myself—and others—to think that I am black and beautiful, or that I am black—and bad, wrong—evil?

After the walk along the Potomac, Robinson invited me to a place called "The Hollywood" to hear some jazz. A young Negro sang with *soul*.

> *Light a little candle*
> *where you are*
> *where you are . . .*

I grew up in Sunday school on that song, and never heard it expressed with such force.

Watching his face, I thought of his integrity, his goodness—as he has defined them. And I realized that we see goodness, integrity, and character only in those who know themselves, who have learned—and apparently it's only through difficulties that one learns to know himself—who one is and what one wants.

I am beginning to see that many blacks truly know them-selves because adversity has forced this self-knowledge upon them.

May 27, 1968

I WENT TO SEE DR. STOLAR AGAIN. "I was a little nervous when I was here before," I told him. "I thought I should ask you, are there any side effects to this medication?"

"No," he said. "None that we have found." The only damage might come from an overexposure to the sun, he told me.

After I take the medication? "You will be very black . . . ," Dr. Stolar said. "You might stay dark for a year."

He said he would order the prescription by telephone whenever I wanted it.

"And you can pick it up at any drugstore?"

"Yes. . . ."

And then I was aware of his ushering me out of his office and into the custody of a large blonde receptionist. She began an endless questionnaire. "Your middle name. . . ."

He said I might stay dark for a year! "I don't have a middle name!" I have but it seemed *so* unimportant.

Standing, aching to escape to the open air, to think a moment. . . .

My entire life would be changed. I would be a different person. My closest friends would not recognize me.

"And where do you work?"

"And your home address?"

". . . And your zip code?"

(You-can-be-quite-dark-in-two-weeks, the doctor had said. Maybe stay that way for a year, so matter-of-fact like, the same as if I had said I had a cold, and he was prescribing some pills.)

"And what is the number of your medical insurance policy?"

"And who recommended you to the doctor?"

I stumbled out into the sunshine, and realized that I not only wanted to be alone, to think of the Experience awaiting me, but that I had desperately wanted to escape the kind of medical person who can't tell a person his life will change without rushing to get the information on which the bill will be based.

It was hot. But there was a gentle breeze cooling the air. *Very black.* The thought kept assailing me. I had thought I would not have to face that. Griffin had said his bones were disappearing, and so I thought that no doctor would want to give the same kind of prescription. Yet this doctor gave it as readily as he would hand out some aspirin.

And where will the turning take place? In a way—because I need to be secretive about this process—I'm somewhat like a pregnant woman wanting to have a child without too many people noticing the Before and After.

June, 1968

Roscoe Dixon has become a steady, constant friend and counselor. He's known since last January about my secret, and each day he encourages me. "I need some *good* sun," I said, and he agreed to drive me to a beach near Annapolis.

He came dressed in shorts and short-sleeved sports shirt, and seemed in a holiday mood. We pinpointed the beach on a map, and were off, with a satchel stocked with boiled eggs, fresh tomatoes, cheese, crackers, and sandwich spread.

We were in my convertible, Roscoe driving, with the top down. He drove too slowly to suit me, but I realized I was out to get the sun and for no other reason, so I relaxed.

As we turned off the Annapolis highway for Sandy Beach, he told me the park was "integrated," but when we arrived amid all the soul brothers I saw that if it were integrated I single-handedly was doing the integrating.

He spread some blankets on the beach and went for an umbrella and cold drinks. I took out my contact lenses and the world turned all misty, hazy—a Seurat blending of uncertain figures and sea and sand. I felt perfectly happy, having cast my lot to fate, and found it as good a provider as any.

By entering into Roscoe's world, I had placed myself in his hands, among his people, at the site of his choosing. I felt strangely, freely, unabashedly liberated from conventional ideas and notions of race and reality. We had temporarily shattered the barriers imposed upon a white woman and a black man. He could have been any color, any age, and I could have been any color, any age.

And so we had that perfect day, and I never felt more content and relaxed and natural and at peace with the world and with myself.

The next morning Roscoe came by.

"I have some good news for you. My brother—he drives a cab—saw me with you. He said, 'Who is that woman? Is she part Indian?' Man," Roscoe added, "he didn't know *what* you were."

He knew this would please me. I am very red-skinned, and Negroes often refer to each other as a "red-skinned Negro" or a "yellow-skinned Negro."

I asked Dixon if he thought the black people at the beach saw me as Negro or white. "They didn't *care*," he said.

"Well," I told him, "one day—before too long—I will take

pills that will make me black. I will be every bit as black as you," I assured him.

"Aw, *no!*" he replied. "You look good the way you are. You can have more respect, as a 'light-skinned Negro.'"

"Roscoe, you miss the entire point! If I want respect I could stay as I am, a Southern white, at the White House."

"We used to see help-wanted ads," he told me, "for light-skinned Negroes."

"But if the Negroes give more respect to the 'light-skinned' Negroes than to the black ones," I protested, "the Negroes are no better than the whites. It's just hopeless."

He pauses, to make his point. "Do you think I'd do the things I do for you if you were *black?*"

"You mean, like doing my washing?"

"I wouldn't do these things for a *black* woman," he says.

"But why?"

"You forget that opposites attract. I like to do things for you, because you are the way you are."

"You mean—white?"

"Yes," he says.

"Roscoe, I'll see you later. I'm getting confused, real confused now."

Laughing heartily, he goes out the door.

The next morning. A soft knock on the door. Roscoe—with a bag of homegrown figs—stands there.

"You want some coffee? Sit down," I suggest. Then: "You can't have meant what you said yesterday—that you think white is more attractive than black."

"Sure, I do. In anything—take a black car; that's not so attractive as a pretty white car. Small babies, still in their cribs, given the choice between black and white playthings, choose the white ones."

"Who told you that?"

"I saw it on TV."

"Who produced the show, who owns all the TV? That's all part of the white Establishment, the white System. You've been brainwashed all your life," I say, smiling. I was without anger, but I wasn't putting him on.

He mentions Malcolm X.

"Remember when I gave you that book?" I asked.

"I still have it—downstairs."

"You took it from my hands as if it were a bomb," I teasingly remind him.

I amaze myself at my effrontery, turning into a teacher of Black Power.

"Malcolm X was a great man. He taught that you don't need to hate whitey, but you should hate the white System, which teaches you white is beautiful and black is ugly.

"At Howard University not long ago—so I've been told by other Negroes—a dark-skinned Negro could never have been accepted into the fraternities and sororities."

"That's right." Then he tells me that in North Carolina a relative of his married a white woman, and some of their children were white and went to a white school and others were "coal burners" and went to a Negro school.

In telling of the white-skinned children he said, "Man, some of those girls had long—" and he makes a caressing wave with his right hand down to his shoulder— "long, 'good' hair." Again he was using the white man's acceptance of beauty, long, silken (no kinks!) hair.

"I'm trying to imagine," I tell him, "what it is to be born a black girl, and all of my life have the people around me accept the idea that being beautiful is to have white skin and long straight hair, 'good' hair as you put it.

"I'm a black girl and I have to spend endless hours of agony having hot combs put on my curly hair to straighten it, and rubbing bleach cream on my skin to lighten it, in order to achieve that national, *white* ideal. And all the while knowing that black men like you think that a white girl is more attractive than a black girl like me. What does this do to me? To my morale? And, if all black people were like you, saying that white cars and white people are more beautiful than black cars and black people, what about *your* morale—if you think that black women are thinking white men are more attractive than black men?"

"Oh," he agrees, matter-of-factly, "the colored people have all these complexes."

At last! I have new *black* eyes!

I first told my optician, Dr. James Maxwell, of my need for them last February, when there was snow on the ground. Since then I have gone a total of forty-eight times to his Maryland offices for fittings, adjustments, tests.

"You will have to choose the color you want," he told me.

"Oh, you can do that," I replied. "I just want—black." I thought all dark eyes were plain black or plain brown, just as I had always seen all Negroes as plain black. I soon learned otherwise.

On my next visit Dr. Maxwell had artificial eyes laid out on a table. I gingerly picked one up. I was amazed at its aliveness. The eyes, row on row, seemed to stare back at me, each with a personality all its own. They were of all gradations, all tones on tones, a mingling of yellow and infinitely drawn lines. "You understand that each contact lens is individually painted," Dr. Maxwell explained.

"How about this?" I pointed to one of the eyes, indicating the color I thought might be appropriate.

"Or this?" he suggested, and it was settled.

Then weeks and weeks of errors, delays. Philadelphia "artists" sent back a sloppy job and Dr. Maxwell would not accept the lenses. When he did accept another "paint job," and mailed the lenses to me, they were lost in the mail!

Weeks more passed. At last Dr. Maxwell called to report that another pair had come in. I drove out to his office, and sitting in front of a table, I pulled up my right eyelid and popped in one of the new lenses, then did the same with the left eye.

Dr. Maxwell had warned me that I would have difficulty adjusting to the new lenses and that for a while I would not have lateral vision. I did not mind that so much, except that now I seemed to have almost no vision at all! Not only that, but my left eye started dripping water like a leaky faucet. The tears would not stop, and Dr. Maxwell, propped up on his stool, looked pleadingly at me. Please, he seemed to be saying: please try to *adjust*.

He couldn't stand my agony any longer. "I think you'll have to take them out," he said at last, "and try to get used to them over a period of time."

As he spoke I looked at the open case for my *blue* lenses, the ones I normally wore. The lens for the right eye lay safely inside the case, but the one for the left eye was missing. "A lens is missing, I've dropped a lens!" I announced. In a sudden reflex action, Dr. Maxwell fell to the floor like a Moslem called to prayer. He was on all fours frantically, if gently, patting the floor. I noted that his technique of looking for a lost contact was no better than mine or the rest of us lens wearers, who have all been in the praying position countless times.

I could not help him search because I was laughing too hard. He looked so ridiculous. Suddenly a possible solution to the puzzle of the missing blue lens occurred to me. "Maybe I've got it in one of my eyes!"

He stood up, his face indicating he was ready to believe anything was possible. "Yes," he agreed. "Well, let's take a look."

I cupped my left hand under my right eye, and with my right

hand squeezed the right lid so that the lens popped out. Then
the same operation with the left eye, and out popped the black
lens that had been riding piggy-back on the missing blue lens
still safe in my left eye.

"No wonder you couldn't 'adjust!' " Dr. Maxwell exclaimed.

"Do you like these eyes?" I had asked Dr. Maxwell.

"They go well with your dark skin," he said.

Since I have determined to make myself black I have studied
the faces of all black people I see. But most people, I am convinced, do not see people, do not see the faces around them.
I have been amazed by the changes within and about me that
others who see me every day have not noticed. None of the
people who were seeing me day after day commented when I
put on dark contact lenses that made my blue eyes black.

"No great accomplishment without great labor," Daddy used
to say. I remembered it now, in the anguish of the two black
contacts, which burn, itch, claw inside my head. I can't see
sideways. I fall down. My head hurts.

Keep them in . . . keep them in. My father's injunction
echoes for me . . . work to get what you want.

July, 1968

I HAVE BEEN to see Dr. Stolar several times now, but I want
also to talk with other doctors before I take medication to turn
my skin black. Some people accept only one doctor's advice,
but I like to see several—especially if I think a matter of life
and death is involved. Besides, I am stepping into a field where

there may be experts, but where what is unknown far outweighs what is known.

I placed a call to the Yale University Medical Center for Dr. Aaron Lerner, who has been described as one of the nation's foremost experts on skin pigmentation. I didn't explain my purpose but asked directly, "Could I come see you *tomorrow* afternoon?" Dr. Lerner said he'd "make it a point" to be in his office, and then as an afterthought said the New Haven airport taxi service was not very good and that he would meet me— "at the Allegheny counter."

It was humid, sunstroke weather when I left Washington and bone chilling and rainy when, an hour later, we set down at the small New Haven airport. I stood by the Allegheny counter, but didn't see anyone who could possibly have been Dr. Lerner, so I called his office.

"He knew the plane would be late and he went on an errand," a secretary told me. "He's been there once and will come back again for you."

"What does he look like?" I asked, turning reporter. "How old is he? Is he about forty, about fifty, about sixty—or what?"

"He's forty-seven," the girl replied.

"Is he tall, short, medium?"

"He's medium. And slender," she said, "and he's got a brown raincoat."

As she spoke I saw the raincoat walking in a door. After we introduced ourselves, he gave me the raincoat, and we walked in the rain to his car. Along the way to the Yale Medical Center he pointed out the sights of the city. It was not until we were approaching his offices that he said his curiosity forced him to ask why I had come to see him.

"I'm going to do what John Howard Griffin did," I told him. "Become a black person—and write about it."

What about the medication psoralen, I wanted to know?

He told me the medical term was trimethyl psoralen, and said the label generally used is "trisoralen." Originally, he said, the medicine came from a plant in Egypt, but when it became difficult to secure, it was produced synthetically.

He explained that skin color comes principally from the dark pigment melanin (produced in cells known as melanocytes, sandwiched between outer and inner skin layers). The quantity and distribution of melanin causes skin to be different colors in different parts of the body, and also plays the major role in the gradation of colors that is found from one individual to another.

The drug psoralen, taken orally before exposure to sunlight or ultraviolet light, steps up the melanin-production process and turns light skin dark.

In albino skin and also in the white splotches of a skin disease called vitiligo, melanin is not produced at all. Psoralen has been used effectively in treating many Negro patients who have the white splotches of vitiligo.

Dr. Lerner said Griffin was the only white person before myself who had taken the medication because *he wanted to be black.*

"Are there any side effects that you know about?"

No, no side effects, Dr. Lerner told me. "When the medicine was first prescribed," he said, "we gave many tests, daily kidney tests, and others, but now we don't bother anymore because we learned they weren't necessary."

He added: "Just as long as you are in good general health. You seem to be. You are, aren't you?" I told him yes.

"And of course your hair is no problem, these days."

The thought of how easily a woman can dye her hair black led me to wonder if Dr. Lerner would not one day produce a mass-marketed pill that will permit a person to choose the color of his skin as easily as a woman chooses the color of her hair.

"Have you ever had any sociological or psychological training?" Dr. Lerner asked.

I said, no, and he continued a train of thought. "Don't you think that some people live with such a poverty of spirit that maybe they need, like a rock on which to stand, some prejudice?" he asked. "Even if you take away one prejudice—and using the most persuasive logic it would be difficult—but even so, they will grab for another. It is something to which some people, seemingly, must cling."

I agreed with him, saying I did not have any answers, that I did not propose to turn black because I loved the Negroes "in general" or the whites "in general"; and that I understood that because we are all humans, we must cope with human deficiencies, foibles, and failures.

My effort, I said, would be an account of how it was for me, for a little while. It would be an exercise in self-detachment and personal surveillance in a black's world, a sublimation of self to make the experience enduring and meaningful.

"I don't propose to *solve* any problems," I said, "but only to *record* a few."

I knew from the way he had phrased his questions that he had become concerned for my safety in an enterprise which involved obvious risks and hazards. My tolerance for the pills seemed of secondary importance to him. Later in his office he wrote out a prescription. He suggested I take one tablet one to two hours before exposing myself to the sun twenty to twenty-five minutes the first day. He advised that I then increase the exposure to one hour. A few days later I was to begin taking two tablets, staying for longer periods in the sun.

"In two or three weeks, you will be *very dark*," he said.

July 9, 1968

A MESSENGER WALKS into my White House office, places an interesting four-by-four-inch square package before me. It is from Dr. Lerner—the medication that will turn my skin black. Airmail. $1.10 in stamps, marked *Personal.* He did not need to send the medicine. He had already written out a prescription. With the package comes the unspoken message: He is with me.

During my visit to New Haven, Dr. Lerner told me he would be vacationing at Cape Cod later in the summer, and suggested I meet Dr. John A. Kenney, Jr., of the Howard Medical School and Freedmen's Hospital here in Washington. Dr. Lerner knew that I would find it comforting, once I started swallowing the pills, to have someone I could call for counseling.

I reached Dr. Kenney by phone, explained that I knew Dr. Lerner, and wanted to talk with him about a personal matter. He said he could drop by my apartment the next afternoon. When he walked in the following day he announced casually that the Bach violin concerto, which was playing softly on the hi-fi, was one of his favorites. Dr. Kenney, in his forties, is a fair-skinned Negro, intensely serious, with a kind expression in his eyes.

I told him I would take psoralen tablets to make myself black, and try to give some meaning to the experience. He listened, without saying anything. Finally when he spoke he said quite simply that he was glad I would do this, and that he would help me in all ways that he could, "both as your doctor and your friend."

I asked Dr. Kenney what he thought of my using a stain in addition to the tablets. "I don't think you'll need one," he said.

He said a skin cream sold at cosmetic counters was very effective in covering up white blotches. And that I might want at some point to apply this to certain areas that failed to respond to the sun and pills.

And, he said, if I should need it, there also was a walnut stain. A patient of his uses potassium permanganate (crystal 0.3 gram tablets) and grinds eight tablets into a pint of water to make the stain.

When he left I realized I had better talk with him again. I hadn't asked whether the patient rubs it in or drinks it!

I have kept the bottle of pills in a place where I could from time to time look at them. When, for one reason or another, I could postpone the swallowing of the first pill, it was like a reprieve. After taking the first pill I waited a couple of hours, then lay in the sun at the Watergate Health Club, and *at that moment* it began to rain! That was one wasted pill, I thought.

That night I could not sleep. The pill, in my imagination, was—in its entirety—sitting inside my stomach and almost had eyes and ears and was observing me! I reached to feel it there, as a pregnant woman would feel the seed within her. I felt (or imagined that I felt) the change that would occur within me because of the change that would be made outside of me.

My last days at the White House! Leaving the job, the security, the pay checks, suddenly I felt suspended, about two feet off the ground. I love the idea of being *free*, and yet it is also an agony, an anxiety, like so much gaseous matter, afloat, no anchor.

I swallowed another pill. Again—to my consternation—it rained. And then the next day, another pill—and the sun shone brilliantly, so that I felt the change was under way. But again I could not sleep. I waked with a severe pain in my right jaw. At first, thinking I had an infected throat, I gargled and sucked on lozenges, but shooting pains persisted. I put that side of my face and jaw on a heating pad, hoping for some relief. Yet I suffered until dawn.

Finally, I remembered Griffin's having told me that his bones were disappearing, and among them, the jawbone. When I had asked if the medication he took in order to become black had caused this bone malady, he said he did not know. Then I realized that all of my pain might have been "in my mind," that I might have been identifying with Griffin.

Another day. I took another pill. Stayed in the sun forty-five minutes. But to me any radical change was imperceptible. Yet in the evening when I went to a cocktail party with my black eyes and what I hoped was darker skin, Angie Duke said, "You look different . . . I hardly recognized you!" Others commented, "My, you have a pretty tan!" Now it is fashionable to be dark, but only if you are really white. That is, a tan is beautiful—if you keep it this side of black.

These days are a time of suspension. There are those around me, those whom I love best, who in a real sense are being rejected by me. I am rejecting them in the sense that I am not allowing them to give me any support, to touch my hand in this moment.

I am now conferring with three doctors, Dr. Lerner, Dr. Kenney, and Dr. Stolar. My idea is that if two heads are better than one, three are better than two. I've been told that doctors have their pride to defend, that one doctor doesn't like your going to another. It may be their pride, but it's my life. I still would like to know more about stains. Maybe after all, if a stain would work, it would be faster, easier, than really turning black. I went back to Dr. Stolar's office and waited two hours before I saw him. My impatience was almost intolerable now. I was sustained by the thought that black women had to wait for busy doctors and everything else in a busy white world.

"I flew up to New Haven to talk with Dr. Lerner," I told

him. "I've started taking the psoralen tablets," and I held out the bottle that Dr. Lerner had sent me. "I'm turning so slowly, and so deeply, that I think I'll be dark a long while," I suggested. He nodded.

Then I betrayed my impatience, blurting that I wanted to turn as quickly as I could and what did he think of my applying a stain on top of my deep tan.

"I've heard of potassium permanganate, that you crush and mix eight tablets to a pint," I told him, "but I've forgotten—do you bathe in it or drink it?"

"You don't drink it!" he replied, breaking into a wide smile (and I was somehow relieved to know that he could). Then he added, quite seriously, "It's . . . poison."

"How many psoralen pills are you taking?" he asked. I said I had started with one, then built up to two.

"Try three," he suggested.

We then discussed a walnut stain. "There is the real thing and the synthetic," he said. "But these stains are *very messy*," he warned. "If your nails get stained they stay black for at least a year. Anything the stain touched would likely *stay black*."

"I could get a tub, take it to an isolated beach, make the mix, bathe in it—and *discard the tub*," I suggested.

"Yes, you'd want to do so," he said.

He telephoned to a pharmacist for a prescription, a stain which I am to rub on a certain part of my arm every two hours to determine how the skin reacts.

I picked up the prescription, flew to New York on business. On the return flight, I rubbed the stain on my right arm for the first time. I was on the shuttle plane surrounded by travelers, performing a very private act in a very public place. I was changing my skin—so I hoped—and no one noticed.

I continued rubbing in the stain every two hours ("but you don't have to get up at night to do it," Dr. Stolar had told me). Two days later I returned to his offices, and waited three hours before seeing him. I wondered if he deliberately was trying to help me by putting my patience to new tests.

The white greasy stain had turned the inside of my right arm a kind of yellowish-red color. It was strange. My skin was not really yellow, not really red. And certainly not black. I had started with a half-ounce jar of stain. "You will need *much* more of it," Dr. Stolar said. Then: "What did you pay for it?"

"I gave a five-dollar bill, and got some change," I recalled.

"I'm supplying the ingredients and they make it up, and I'll tell them to give you a better price," he said. "It has to form overnight," he continued, making it sound like yogurt, or yeast for bread. He said I would now get a large jar, and that I should rub the stain all over my face, arms, and legs—over all exposed areas. He told me I didn't need to rub it on the inside of my hands, the palms. I knew that much already.

Day after day, I swallow the pills, put on the stain, and expose my body in the awful 90-degree humid weather. I am a "high yaller," not black. One day at the Watergate swimming pool, I use the pay phone to call Dr. Stolar, suggesting that maybe the sun is melting the stain? Or that the stain is only acting as a shield to keep the sun from having full force? He said no, he wouldn't think that either was the case.

Still, I don't like the color I have with the stain. I will not use the stain anymore—the sun will give me the color. And perhaps I'm overanxious? It's patience that's required! I've been like a person standing over a kettle, and the water won't boil if one is too anxious.

Still, the comments I get are reassuring.

At the bank, a woman teller: "Oh, what a tan." (Pause) "It looks so—*deep*."

At the health club: "My, you have a good tan." (Pause) "You are almost *black!*"

Several of the women around the pool have asked: "Were

you in Florida?" One woman said: "I saw you yesterday. Today you are an entirely *different color.*"

I think this is revolutionary. I swallow pills, others go to Florida.

But as my skin changes slowly, I feel that I am preparing myself psychologically.

I called Jack Kenney in Houston, where he was attending a Negro medical convention. I told him I wanted my skin to change more rapidly. "Should I go to Puerto Rico?" I asked Dr. Kenney.

He said, "I think that would be interesting."

I telephoned Dr. Lerner at Cape Cod and he asked my opinion about the Presidential campaigns. I am so little interested in politics (the subject of my life for the past three years!) that he could have asked me about the other side of the moon. I told him I'm dark but wish to be *black.*

He suggested another medication, 3 to 5 per cent Zetar in aquaphor (one half-pound jar) to be rubbed into the skin before sun exposure. He explained that a light coating of this— "take a tissue and rub off any excess, before going out"—will permit the sun to penetrate the skin more readily.

"Also, I imagine you need a stronger sun," he said. "After all, Washington is still pretty far north."

"I thought I'd go to Puerto Rico."

"Yes, that sounds good."

Puerto Rico

Dawn—and without brushing my teeth I pull on a bathing suit, run only a few feet to the sea. I run along the shore. I talk back to the sand and sky and say, Oh, world, I can't get you close enough! On the beach my eyes wander off to the distance. I relive the past, uncover old secrets, bare old wounds, once again experience pain, joy, and by recreating a life that is in only one sense gone, I am blessed with a longer, yet another life.

I lie on the beach, I sit on the beach, I walk along the beach, and as the days turn I see man in his variety, man in his gradation of colors, all beautiful, the fair-skinned blond to the blackest Negro. All blend in with the sand, the sea, and all live here harmoniously. I hold a child from Trinidad, dressed in pink dotted swiss, with a bow in her kinky, plaited hair. She smiles, then runs away.

My first day at Lutece-by-the-Sea, I met a Negro, Jim Hamilton from New York, with an Afro beard and hair and attractive loose African shirt. I was lying in the sun, soaking in the color, and Hamilton passed by: "You'll lose it all in a few days, back in the city," he said.

"No," I replied. "I'm going to keep it."

He laughed, and his face suggested he thought I was a silly white woman. But he wanted to talk, to know who I was, where I lived, and after a bantering exchange, he wrote out his name

*and address in New York and gave it to me, and I was sorry
when he told me he was returning home that afternoon. "Call
me if you get to New York," he said, with casual ease.*

*The sun fades. In a community-shower stall I try to remove
the layers of dirt-tar-ointment from my skin which I once
pampered with twenty dollars per ounce of moisture cream.
But a residue of the medicated lotion mixed with sand remains.
And the hair I once piled high for ambassadorial receptions
now is peasant's hair, coarse, neglected, combed straight back
with nervous fingers.*

*There is a ritual: dawn and to the beach; midmorning I
walk four blocks to Café Ortiz for cafe-con-leche y pan and
then, often to a sad jukebox tune, "Cuando no estas a mi lado,
corazon" ("When you are no longer here, dear one"), I swallow two make-me-black pills, and return to the sun. Again, in
the afternoon, two, sometimes three more pills, depending on
my mood.*

*Walking on the beach. An English girl with her mother stops
to chat. "How long have you been here?" she asks, then, peering closely, "Or, do you live here?" Another girl approaches.
She is perhaps nineteen, with long hair that falls into her eyes,
and pallid skin that seems dully impervious to the sun. "It's
disgusting," she announces and I wait for her to continue. "I'm
using Coppertone, too" (both of us have plastic bottles in our
hands), "but I can't get your color!" She lifts my spirits by
exclaiming, "You are black!"*

*"Que hora es?" I ask Ernesto, a black Puerto Rican who is a
general fix-it man. He wears a fine Elgin, but it does not keep
time. He grins, admires his showpiece watch, then calls me
"Negrita . . . negrita" (black one). I put my arm against his
to compare color. We both smile to note that there is no
difference.*

*Each evening, as I sit on a small terrace watching clouds
paint closing-day pictures, a tall sun-wrinkled woman guest who*

teaches school in Philadelphia nods on her way to her cabin. For three evenings, she nods and smiles. On the fourth, she pauses to say, "My God, you are black!"

I ask: "How can you tell in the dark?"

"You glow!" she replies.

Paulina, whom I knew in Colombia, and who is married to a Puerto Rican, comes to take me for a drive. Seeing me, she exclaims, "You are black!" She inspects me with something akin to horror. "You must see a doctor! You are burned, you must see about those blisters on your feet." I am afraid, however, to see a doctor. He might tell me to stay out of the sun, to stay off my feet.

"Too much sun isn't good for you," Paulina says with some agitation, sounding like my mother. "It causes skin cancer."

As she drives through the rain forest, repeatedly warning me of the danger of the tropical sun, I keep my mind on the scenery, and my fears under tight rein.

The seventh day. Once more I walk along the beach, journey back in time, to other days, other places, other climates, when only the elements were real, the snow, rain, cold, heat, always running to extremes. And in those days we were ignorant but spirited, fighting back, facing into the wind, taking on the cold, zestful, alive, undaunted. Back from the seashore, I bathe and close the shutters and remove my loose shift and stand before the mirror—and gasp in horrified disbelief! The skin, the precious, beautiful black skin, my labor of love, literally hangs like falling wallpaper from around my eyes. Frantically, tearfully, I grab for the pieces, try to paste them back into place, to restore the black face that was.

As I sit looking at that face with pale, accusing eyes—self-indicted as miserable, ugly, unloving, and unlovable, not myself, not another, a no-body, a no-thing—the eyes condemn me, no longer able to see the person I have destroyed, only this unraveled, molting monster I have created.

I throw the old wet bathing suits in a bag, along with the huge jar of tar ointment (and why am I keeping that?) and the suntan cream and the pills, and go downstairs to pay my bill. After failure, there's always flight.

Lucette, the petite French owner, follows me to the taxi. "Never saw color like yours!" she's saying. "You stayed only a few days—and got black."

Four hours waiting, the flight back, the long bus ride from Baltimore's Friendship Airport to Washington. It is past midnight when I get into my apartment, my body feeling too heavy for my feet, the hurt of failure too heavy for my heart.

I, black woman, white woman—human, female—ache. I am too alone! I envelop myself in a blanket of self-pity. I am ravaged by a sense of great loss—and weakness. I feel I have betrayed the pledge that women make: to keep our secrets, our understanding of deep mysteries, nobly and undefiled—because we know pain and we welcome pain.

The next morning Dr. Kenney came to see me. "Haven't you ever peeled before?" he asked curiously. I never had. I had absorbed a strong sun in Peru, on the equator, and Saudi Arabia, Greece, Morocco, Algeria, not to mention Texas. But the common experience of peeling *had escaped me. I had feared that the medication, plus hours of concentrated sun, had led to a decomposition of my skin.*

"Don't worry," the doctor said, "Don't you see that underneath that peeled layer you are still black?" And he added, "You'll pass."

To reassure myself, I put my arm against his. He is Negro, but I am still darker.

Part II

HARLEM

Harlem

THE ALARM SOUNDS AT 6 A.M. I put on a simple cotton dress and flat shoes, insert the black "eyes," and tie a kerchief over my hair, which hasn't been washed since before Puerto Rico. And I pack—the same bag I've always handled with insouciance I now pack with portentous dread. Harlem, only four nonstop bus hours away, seems distant and awesome, a land of menace and fear. I keep in wordless touch with the seat of my courage. Harlem, I tell myself, assuming the logic of a tour guide, is still in *this* country (linked by telephones, telegrams) . . . still in Manhattan! We might call it a city within a city, not like other shanty black communities, on the Other Side of Town. There are drugstores . . . yes, you can be sure of that! And yes, the natives speak our language.

The double-decker rolls along, must be hitting seventy. Am going by bus because it seemed foolish to *jet* to a ghetto. The ticket costs $9.15, and I have only twenty dollars left in my purse. I go with the necessity of finding a place to live, and a job, goals I've imposed upon myself within the *time* that the money will last.

Soon be there! In that ghetto that everyone wants to "study," and no one wants to understand, that largest black metropolis in the world. I have never seen it except in a cluttered, symbol-ridden mind's eye. I've read the papers, heard the reports of *violence in the streets*, of a community peopled by Dickensian elements, drunks, pushers, thieves, murderers, dope addicts, the deprived, the predator. "Maybe one will grab me?" And, "He could be 'down with his habit!'" I've heard an addict will do anything, rob, steal, murder his own mother—anything to get money to buy dope. I build for myself a pantheon of villains.

In Harlem I will no longer carry my identity card that has always provided me with special status: white American, member of *the* club. I will be going to a black country, where in all directions, uptown, downtown and crosstown, there will be nothing but black faces. I will no longer be the person I have always been, and to enter into this new world I will have to ask to be accepted. I will be knocking on the ghetto door, beseeching: let me come in, accept me as one of you, a black among blacks.

And the militants? The Black Panthers and the Rams and those who are armed and ready to burn it *all* down, those who want to kill a white for every black that's ever been killed. . . . If they learn I'm "white" passing for a "black"—what might they do? I've heard that the black militants are as bad as the Ku Klux Klan, very nationalistic, out to kill. And they want the black world kept for the blacks, without any whitey snooping around. Especially, whitey the reporter, whitey the writer— paid agent of the white Establishment.

Yes, I've packed all of my old fears, right in with the nylons and hairbrush. I'm not *supposed* to go there. . . . The white man says the black man is a beast and marauder, he will rape you, rob you, he is mean as the devil (you know the devil has got to be black). This mythology makes me a trespasser; I go where I have no "right" to be; my world won't condone it; my people won't understand it.

So the bus moves toward Dante's inferno. No, not Dante's but Claude Brown's, James Baldwin's, Billie Holiday's. And through my roiling mind: *Abandon All Hope Ye Who Enter Here.* No telling what's going to happen to a good white woman like me going to that place! And *why* should I be afraid?

The bus wheels turn, and I talk to myself in a monologue of reassurance that fear doesn't accompany me. I summon the memories of my going to live in a junk with the Chinese, of floating down the Amazon, 2,000 miles on a tug, the only woman, not afraid. Nothing physical ever frightened me—so why the big deal?

Why had I not wanted to get on this bus?

Why do I fear entering this black enclave as I have never feared any other place?

Because there are signs you don't see, big, lurid signs all over this country. They shout out: you are white, you are a white woman and have no business going into that ghetto—it belongs to *them.* And the rest, *all* the rest, belongs to you.

The bus arrives; the passengers scatter, and I am in the streets of midtown Manhattan, with the hurtling taxis and people all dressed up in their special survival suits.

Into the subway. Do I want a Lexington? A Seventh? It's Uptown, I know that much, and I give myself to the first screaming mass of machinery that whips me uptown. Now I sit in a sea of black faces. I must begin, but where? I do not know where to go.

I turn to one black face, a woman's. I shout over the roaring clatter. "Do you know a guest house . . . ?"

"Not in Harlem. I live in the Bronx," she explains.

I get off at 125th Street and climb toward the light. Here before me is the ugly, awful, open wound that is Harlem. Early afternoon. I see the nodding, bobbing addicts, the drunks swinging empty bottles around their heads like lassos, crap shooters, pushers, and strewn through the streets like mines on a battlefield, the broken, jagged liquor bottles.

The black scar on our white conscience: the dilapidated houses with kids and mamas and old men in postures of idleness, hanging out of the windows, out on the fire escapes, sitting on garbage cans, filling up the broken-down stoops. A truck stops, and I can hardly believe what I see. A derelict in a mindless act deliberately places his body under the wheels. Has he yielded to the heat, to dope or drink, or to his private griefs? By chance some men shooting craps see him and shout a warning to the driver.

Too many sights, sounds, smells swarm over me at once. The row on row of liquor stores and bars, the prostitutes out in coveys trying to "turn a trick." At 116th, I see them climbing into cars when men stop at street signals.

All and none of it fits together, because I can't identify, I can't say this part reminds me of Paris, this is a little like Rome, over here like Tokyo.

It isn't a big place and it isn't a small place, and one can walk all over it. Where is a hotel? A tourist hotel? Or, am I the first white single female *tourist* ever to hit this part of town?

I stop a woman in a nurse's uniform. "Do you know of *any* hotels around here?"

She replies, "Not around here!" so forcefully that I keep walking—faster.

A few blocks later, I ask about the old Theresa, remembering it as the place where Castro went "uptown" when he visited the United Nations in 1960. "It's not operating any more as a hotel," I am told.

"What about that hotel, the Wilthon?" I point down Seventh, while talking with a motherly type. "Do you think I might stay there—*just for one night?*"

Oh, she replies, that would be "more than enough."

I keep walking, clinging to the thought that there's always room for one more, always a room at the inn, just the right place is going to turn up. I pass the Black Panther headquarters, in an area where Harlem again presents a scene of despair and debasement: liquor stores, bars, and more liquor stores and bars. Churches, faith healers, beauty shops, small stores, small cares—no business that you'd term "black business." And the people walking around imprisoned in an open-air jail, as if the place doesn't belong to them and they, too, are transient here.

I can't see Harlem the way I've seen other "foreign" places, where I've sat in a public park and let the sights, sounds, smells—and atmosphere—come to me. In those places, I have sat until I felt a part of the whole varied stream of life. But Harlem is different. To begin with, there's no place to sit, for even the garbage cans are already occupied by weary squatters.

I can't imagine how I could see Harlem unless I had also seen New Delhi . . . the slums of Lima . . . Rio . . . Hong Kong. Here in Harlem is a special kind of "poverty," poverty amid affluence. In *our* slums the poor drink *diet* colas. And they go to the "poorhouse" in an automobile. Poorness here is of a different, more dismal, more poignant and paradoxical texture.

The streets are lined with cars; there is money flashing everywhere. I stop for coffee at Richard's on Seventh Avenue. The poorest-looking derelict drunk sits on a counter stool next to me and orders a plate supper which he does not eat. Later he orders tea, then forgets to drink it, but he puts down a dollar tip. The drunk is going out the door when Richard, the owner, calls, "You forgot to drink your tea." The drunk waves to him, as if he'd forgotten an unwanted scrap of paper.

It's not that the people are starving to death (my mind conjures up the thin stacks of bones strewn like debris, those dead and dying of India). And the people are not even *dirt* poor, like the poor of Paraguay, who live on the dirt and can extract edible roots from it. No, it is rather that here in Harlem they are reminded that they are the poorest of the poor in an affluent society because they have been denied their *dreams* and the American promise is worthless, a lie.

Walking, walking . . . I feel a special gray death—like the heavy Peruvian fog, *garua*—hanging over Harlem, hanging over my spirits. Every person here appears *condemned*—he has no way out, he may shout, scream, plead, but his voice won't be heard. Yet in this prison, life is lived with a kind of wild zest. I note the lively way of walking. I hear the gutter language ("that fucking man took my fucking money"), the profanity blending with the warmness and hurt in the voices of Aretha Franklin and James Brown blasted through loudspeakers from record shops, two and three to a block.

I walk these streets, and remember they were once the good-time mecca for the white "swells" who made the trip uptown to hear Negro musicians and singers and to watch Negro dancers in *white-owned* nightclubs. These streets, from which Josephine Baker fled to Paris, Paul Robeson to Moscow, Lena Horne to Broadway, now spawn a curious breed: young dandies who've spent hundreds of dollars on their suits and saunter along in coveys, their vanity and pride assuaged by the flamboyant colors, slacks, sweaters and alligator shoes, everything matching in the same brilliant yellow, red or green.

I am here, but where am I to go? I need a sign, like Nice Clean Room Just Put Up For You. Or a large hand stretched out, God's handwriting on some wall, or across the sky. I remember I'd met *a* Negro from New York City—Jim Hamilton—in Puerto Rico. Why hadn't I thought of him before? Why hadn't I written him, *used* him—isn't that why we Americans go around being friendly in bars and airplanes, so we'll always have a friend of a friend, in case we're stuck in some God-forsaken place? I don't even know in what part of New York he lives. It occurs to me that all Negroes don't have to live in Harlem. But already the name of Jim Hamilton appears like Constantine's vision—*In Hoc Signo*—emblazoned across my sky. One good friend, that's all you need. He'll know a family and they'll take me in. Just get to him and explain everything!

I'm feeling as confident as if in Paris I'd encountered a Frenchman who understood my French. Yes, sir, I'm beginning to feel I can find my way now. I go to a phone booth at 125th and Seventh, check the directory, and find the name and number. I put in a dime, the coins runs through and I get the dime back. I try again, and get my dime back again. I go to an adjacent phone booth; the glass pane is out and the horns and sirens and street talk come swarming into the booth with me. Another dime and the machine swallows it. Frustrated, silently pleading, I bang the phone slightly, then more furiously. I try another dime, and again the machine engulfs it and still no dial tone. I walk around the booth and approach a black man standing there. He's plainly proud of his African heritage, wearing an Afro natural hair style, a beard, and almost blindingly bright attire (purple slacks, kelly-green pullover).

"How do you get the phones to work?"

Studying me as he would a lost child he replies, "Get two nickels, put the first one in very slowly, then put the second in very, *very* slowly."

Is he kidding? It isn't supposed to be a game of chance, but a telephone, and Bell has promised to take quarters, nickels, or dimes, indiscriminately.

"Well, I don't have nickels."

"Go get some," he replies. Then eyeing my suitcase: "You can leave that with me. I'll watch it."

Does he think I'm crazy? Stalling for time, I ask his name.

"My name is Prince," he tells me, proudly. "I am beautiful. That is because I am real."

"Do you know of a hotel around here where I might stay?"

"You can't stay around here!" he says. "Even I wouldn't go into these hotels. Keys won't work. Men walking in your room *all hours of the night*! And you'll be eaten alive by the bugs!"

Convinced I have no choice but to leave my bag with Prince, I walk off, get some change, put the nickels in the phone, get a dial tone, but there's no answer when I dial Jim Hamilton's number.

I start again on my pursuit of a room for the night. Four hours I've walked now, always with suitcase in hand. I find myself standing in front of the Douglas Hotel, at St. Nicholas Avenue and 151st.

I walk up the steps. Fatigue and hopelessness have made me indifferent, and I no longer care if only pimps, prostitutes, and pushers inhabit the place. I'm too tired. They must take me in!

A black man stands before a glass window and hands a bill to the cashier. He turns and motions to a woman, lingering in the shadows, and together they mount a flight of stairs leading from the small vestibule. I go to the window, tell the man I have come from Washington, that "a friend" recommended the hotel. I feel desperate, and I want him to read me right.

"Are you alone?" Yes. He pushes out a registration card for me to sign. "What kind of room do you want?" *Any* room, I mutter. My one hope is that the key will be my key. I pay the glassed-in man five dollars in advance—no one takes the bag—no one shows me the room—and walk alone up the flight of stairs. I turn down a dark corridor on the third floor and enter a room in total darkness. I fling myself across the bed, exhausted but grateful, and half doze off. Gradually, I become conscious that a heavy man, no, many heavy men have been on the mattress before me, and they have worn a niche in it, and that my sleeping there is like having fallen into a hammock. I am repelled by the thought, but too weary to care, and sink into the slump of the mattress as though it were my mother's arms.

The hallway creaks. Someone's heavy tread. I hear the words again: *"Men walking in your room all hours of the night!"* A door opens. I listen, my heart pounding, thinking it is my door. But no, the stranger enters the community bathroom next door. I start breathing again.

My God! Might I have just as well delivered myself to a prison? Two or three hours later, I get up and try to peer out the window, but outside there is only a blank wall. And inside the dark wallpaper seems to draw in like a collapsing bellows that is closing in on me. I can't breathe. I must escape. In the streets, like any Harlemite, I can move and maneuver, I have a chance. Still in the same dress, I stuff my swollen feet into my shoes and go back into the streets.

I stop at a phone booth to try to reach Jim Hamilton. Again, no answer. Finally I go into the Hide-A-Way, a small eatery of bedroom size and coziness with a few cramped booths in the rear and a row of counter stools. An easy repartee between waitresses and customers indicates that the same people regularly patronize it.

Several times during my supper of pork chops and collard greens, I try to telephone Hamilton and finally reach him at his home, on St. Nicholas. We arrange to meet at the Bowery Bank corner at 10:30 P.M. It is a six-block walk from the Hide-A-Way and I am glad at last to see him, standing there at St. Nicholas and 137th, waiting for me. "My God, you got black!" he remarks. He is perhaps thirty-six, with Afro beard, and natural, fuzzy coif. He is wearing dark trousers and a striped white-and-black jacket. He hails a taxi—the first I had been in during the eternity of the day. We drove to a small bar on 125th. Jim was completely in charge as he gave the driver a handsome tip and escorted me inside the dimly lit bar.

A man greeted us with a heavy Spanish accent, indicating that if we took a table at the back we could at a later hour enjoy the floor show. Jim seemed irritated at finding himself, a proud Afro, in this club that had changed from All Soul ("It used to be a Negro place!" he told me) to one with a *latino* beat. Like many other Harlemites, he resented that his ground was being usurped, this time by the Puerto Ricans. He considered whether we'd go or stay. Finally he motioned me to the bar.

Hamilton undoubtedly foresaw only a pleasant, uncomplicated interlude, with beer in hand, and a superficial conversation. Perhaps he had experienced a difficult day as an assistant school superintendent and felt, as any hard-pressed man at the end of the day, that he wanted to be greeted by a quiet, smiling female with no problems of her own.

What he got was my frustration and fear and thwarted plans and painfully innocent notions spilled all over his nice manner and his composure. I told him everything, adding "I need your help."

Just as frankly he replied that I would not get it. He let me know that he and others like him were sick and tired of white liberals coming to "study" and help the Negroes. "You help as long as *your needs* hold out, and then when you've eased a guilty conscience your help is finished."

He said that not for one second would he condone such romantic notions as a desire to go poking my nose into his friends' lives "to discover more of your untruths." And he added, "No, no indeed, I won't open up any of my friends' closets—for your inspection!"

"Jim . . . I want a closet of my own." I was being womanly— logical in the way that so infuriates a man. But I recognized in Jim Hamilton the indignant black man who is sick of the white liberal who seeks self-identity through little pitying acts of condescension, running up to Harlem to make himself more compatible with his conscience.

He'd been perfectly willing to drink a quiet beer with me as someone who was only female. Now he saw me as the activist and he hated me, hated me for all that whiteness represented, a sluggish callousness, yet with ego bent on action and the "right" to lead the struggle, to guide the Negro, and with the additional right to be cheered, recognized, for having always done "so many good things" for the colored folk. He hated me because he now saw me as part of the System that has permitted America to concern itself with poverty, discrimination, and deprivation around the world without applying its vast resources to sickness at home.

Well, stay out! Jim was saying to me.

"Jim," I told him, "if I had only come to drink a beer with you, that would have been all right. Or, if rather than seeing me on the day I arrived in Puerto Rico, *white*, you had seen me later, with dark skin and black lenses, then you would have accepted me. But you have raised the huge Off Limits sign only because I was frank with you, only because I have told you I want to educate myself, and *to write* about it."

He was off on another tirade. "No, no! Your timing is just *too right*. Just at the time Harlem closes itself to the white press, you come up, to make your 'study,' no doubt to report on 'Negro violence,' while the violence against black people is taken for granted, like the weather!

"Why don't you write about the System and the Establishment? Why don't you reveal who controls all the importation of narcotics in this country? Why don't you write how the mass media perpetuate the evils of slavery?

"You can't understand me, you can't understand the man or the woman of Harlem because *you* can't have known the special burden of being black in this country. You can't have known the person you're trying to write about when he was a child of five, a child of ten—and all of the years, or all of the evils of the society that can oppress a man, make him so ashamed that he is among the oppressed, rather than the oppressors!"

Jim's rage struck me in the face and heart. Feebly I tried to defend my position: "I'm not trying to understand or write about *your* life, but only to live awhile in Harlem and relate *my* experiences."

He again repeated that no "truths" could come from that.

Even as we were leaving, his resentment spilled over once again. "Why did you have to pick on me to help you?"

"Because I knew you'd be the way you are—the black militant. I'm glad I wasn't wrong."

But when he left me back at the hotel I felt more despondent than when I had met him.

After I'd climbed into my hammocklike slump, I knew that Jim was right in his accusations of whitey. Brotherly love seemed so hopeless. The past so strewn with sins. How rise above them? Then I remembered the beauty of Malcolm X's growth and his rising above hatred of a man because of his color. On his pilgrimage to Mecca in 1964 he discovered he could break bread with a blond, blue-eyed Moslem and be treated as a brother. The trip convinced him that skin color is less important than point of view; that awareness, not pigment, is crucial. Now that it was too late I remembered the final conviction of Malcolm X and wished I had quoted that to Jim: *You can hate the System*—Malcolm had told the black people in his last days—*but there's no need to hate the person*. My thoughts race wildly from present to past and back again this first night in Harlem.

None of my family, indeed, *no one knows where I am*. Time clings like fungus to my skin, to my being. At first I listen to the noises. The creaking footsteps that seem to walk across your guts. The sirens that wail endlessly. Another overdose? Another stabbing? A .38 in the chest? A murder? A fire? All night the sirens tell the story of Harlem—a cacaphony of heart-ache, tragedy, trouble—and then the silence.

I listen to the silence, searching for noises I can identify.

I tug at memories to ease the loneliness: a child sitting in church (three times on Sundays), and the preacher, running up and down the pulpit, pumping both his arms, doing his gymnastics, down on his haunches, telling it right to me, "You can depend on Jesus. . . ." And I'm listening, and hear him still: "If you are sick, if you are sick, if you need Him real bad— He will come get in bed with you!" And that room in Manaus in Brazil? Wasn't that worse? The dollar room, the jungle all around, the strange, dark-faced men in that cheap hotel, one single girl, the temperature soaring . . . the mosquitoes, one dirty sheet, the room faced against a wall, no breeze, not an ounce of air. Was there a design that night that prepared me for this night and now told me that this night also would end?

Lying in my dark cell I remember the memo I had composed several months ago about how I proposed to go into the ghetto and feel the pulse and find out why all *those* people felt so estranged from our way of life, and even from their *own* people—those who were like us, the common-sense people.

The only people who can help me now are the residents of the ghetto. I will have to knock on their doors and they will have to take me in. None of my Negro friends who live in white cities can reach out to me. I have Negro friends (I am one of those modern white people who has been able to say "some of my best friends are . . ."), but they are "white people" who happen to have black skins, and they cannot help me.

The next morning: My feet are swollen into enormous clubs, misshapen and unsightly. Blisters sprout like rampant mushrooms, covering my heels, soles and toes. I try to get out of bed. I cannot walk. I find myself down on my hands and knees on the dirty floor. Crawling, I gather up my bra, panties, dress, shoes, and sitting on the floor, I dress myself. I test one foot, then the other. The left is stronger. I use it to hobble down the stairs and onto the streets.

Early morning, but record shops that stay open past midnight are again amplifying soul music. I listen to one of the jukebox tunes, "Down on the Ground". . . . Talk to me, brother! He's looking up at the birds, the jukebox shouted, wanting to fly away with his spirit, but he's hemmed in, grounded—and I'm thinking, yes, that's how I feel, *buried alive!* And yet I have only to step to a phone booth, put in a dime, dial a number and tell the operator, put this on my Washington number. It is that simple. My spirit could fly away. I can so easily escape, escape the reality that no person in Harlem can escape . . . the reality of being a black American.

Last evening, before meeting Jim Hamilton, I had walked into the Hide-A-Way café in a condition that I will term as one of the most desperate in my life. Never had I felt so miserable. Later, as I walked forlornly out of the Hide-A-Way, after my supper of pork chops, Longus Moore, the owner, standing by the cash register, exclaimed, "You've got the prettiest color I've ever seen!" He startled me as much as if he'd plucked out my heart. *Prettiest color!* I knew that Negroes praised and highly rated certain color variations and hues, and that Langston Hughes had sung paeans to a variegated group of "colored" beauties: sepia thrill, brown-sugar lassie, caramel treat, honey-gold baby, coffee and cream, chocolate treat, walnut-tinted, cocoa brown, rich cream-colored to plum-tinted black, cordial, licorice, clove, cinnamon, honey-brown dream. . . . Was Moore speaking as a chocolate to a caramel? Or, was he on to my game?

"Please, do me a favor," he said, "Come back again, just so I can admire that *color!*"

Now as I try to make my way to the Harlem Hospital emergency ward, I am drawn to the Hide-A-Way. After I've ordered grits, Moore comes to my side, jokingly asks if he can move "this thousand dollars," indicating my handbag I have on one of the stools beside me.

We talk very simple talk. It is not at all like the inflamed rhetoric I'd engaged in the night before with Jim Hamilton.

Moore is a totally black Negro: not one of the modern pretty boys, but Negroid all the way, the lips, the nose, and the eyes. He is about forty-five years old, rather short, balding, sturdy, almost pudgy.

"You can't walk there, with those feet," he tells me when he learns I am on the way to Harlem Hospital. He goes for his car while I pay my bill. I hobble out to find him sitting in a robin's-egg blue, late-model Cadillac convertible. I sit silently as he drives down St. Nicholas Avenue. At the red light on 135th, he studies me, and senses my aloneness. He knows I am in need, although he cannot immediately pinpoint what my needs are.

The red light is brief, but it is long enough for his words: "I will help you."

The words are so simple, somehow so sharp-edged—for the good can hurt as much as the bad, sometimes more—that I want to shout, this is not fair! I came here to know you for what you are, you beast, you black, black, black man! And you are ugly to me. You are a nigger. And you feel sorry for me. You are pitying me, you are, Christ in heaven, you are loving me! It's not supposed to be like that! You're telling me you don't care if you ever see me again, but that you will help me, that you will help me no matter what my trouble, no matter what I've done. You are my friend? God, how I need you, how I want you.

My face is buried in my hands; the tears are coming. And I feel helpless and stripped naked, stripped bare of those myths

I've worn like crown jewels—that white is right, that black is wrong. Moore takes the scales away, he alone, and he does it with four words: *I will help you.* Help me? How often can one help another? How often does one try?

"It's nothing to be ashamed of to run out of money . . . ," he tells me, presuming that I need money (or might need money before I find a job). He will loan me money, he wants to see me out of my dark miserable hotel room, and he offers to help me find an apartment! *No talk of my snooping around in closets, looking for untruths!* "I'm not including myself in any of this," he makes plain. He is doing it simply because he wants to help me, "whether I ever see you again or not, it doesn't matter."

I have opened the car door to get out and go into the hospital. "But why? Why? Why would you do this? Why would you want to help me this way?"

"I can't explain it myself," he says, adding: "But you must have done something right—someplace, sometime."

I enter the Harlem Hospital emergency ward. A woman screams, and a nurse says it's a miscarriage. I see a man wheeled by on a stretcher, his head badly mangled.

I study the faces and am startled by the agony and grief etched on them. This is precisely the way Goya and Daumier had painted the poor, the destitute, the forgotten people who have suffered beyond human capacity to endure, but somehow have gone on enduring as "faceless" women and men.

Obviously there are hundreds more patients than the emergency ward can handle. We are all reduced to the level of cogs arrayed for inspection on an assembly line. You're bleeding to death? Giving birth? Got an overdose? A broken leg? Shot in the groin? Stand here, move over, wait your turn, fill out this form, next group, please. Keep moving.

How can requirements for "emergency" treatment take so much of one's time and energy? At my side stands a man in his seventies, whose car had been hit by a truck at 7 A.M. that same morning. His face is frozen in pain and he holds on to his neck, which I imagine has been broken. He has been waiting for more than two hours, and still no X-rays have been taken. Over and again we both give answers to the same questions: your father's name, your mother's name, your age, address, zip code, telephone number, place of business, and all those questions aside, still more: your religion.

And *"How did you get here?"* And the old man's patient, long-suffering reply: "I rode a bus."

At last I hear my name called and go into a cell-like examination room. I have been moving in a sea of blackness, the black faces of women, men and children on all sides of me. Seeing a white face in the small examination room, I am momentarily startled, wondering what's he doing in here— among *us colored people?* Then I recall that a number of Columbia University interns work at Harlem Hospital and that this near-albino white (and whites by now were all beginning to look *sickly* pale) must be one of them. I sit down. He seems eager to hear that I have a dramatic case to present. I begin explaining my malady. His wrath descends. "You mean you came in here to show me your feet!"

His tone indicates he is a busy, important professional and he might deign to give me five minutes but only if I promise to die from, let's say, a knife in my side, two or three bullets, a miscarriage or at least an overdose of dope. But where have I gotten the idea that I am a *person?* That is stepping out of my place, even for a Harlem nigger. He stares incredulously as though I have been uppity in coming here with such a minor complaint, and I sit dumbly, feeling more prisoner than patient.

"Rip off those bandages!" he orders, and I have no other recourse but to comply. Why have I come in here? I grit my teeth for the punishment he imposes. And why does he talk to me in a tone that indicates he hates me *for even existing?*

"*You people*," he lectures me, "should bathe more often. Your feet are *dirty!*" He says there is nothing wrong with my feet. "*Just* blisters." Again he utters the stern injunction that I must bathe myself and my feet, *every day.* He gives me no treatment or medication. I leave wondering if he talks to all "colored people" as he had talked to me, indicating that we were all dirty, somehow less than human.

Another day, and I am on the streets again. Since I have no "home," no friends in Harlem, the streets are becoming my home, the people my people. On the corner of 137th and Lenox I see a woman drink from a whisky bottle. Her man sits beside her and assists her in her drinking, and she mutters about someone always trying to mind other peoples' business "when folks got enough to worry 'bout theirselves." I cross the street and see now a man drinking from a whisky bottle. Yet this is not all. There are bright-eyed children, laughing, jumping ropes, playing ball.

Somehow, despite my throbbing feet, I keep going. Now, walk the streets with me. You see the old brownstones up close. Nearly all were built in a spurt of energy that lasted from the 1870's through the first decade of the twentieth century. You see streets littered with garbage, children chasing balls amid the cars; the drunks, the whores, the junkies, pushers, gamblers, pimps, the big, ugly black scar on your white existence; you don't want to think, you look away. Now up close you see that those old brownstones that once wore the look of middle-class respectability now wear the neglect of corrupt, absentee ownership. The stoops are broken, covered

with derelicts and debris so thick it's like the excrement of the
guano birds, piles and piles of it.

Climb the steps, go into the dark corridors. See the mass of
slum dwellers living out their existence with the rats, the bed-
bugs, and the empty liquor bottles. Squeeze into one of the
tiny rooms, not living quarters so much as a cell, a cell worse
than you'd get if you were sentenced to jail—and you're supposed to pay twenty-five dollars a week for that!

Keep walking, along 135th, the long block crossing from
Lenox over to Seventh Avenue. Not much along here now
except trashy stores, but in 1920 this was Harlem's main
thoroughfare, with an almost solid block of houses and stores
owned by St. Philips' Protestant Episcopal church.

Here's the site of Father Divine's famous eatery. During
the depression he brought his Kingdom of Peace right down
to earth by opening restaurants all over Harlem where a poor
man could eat a fine chicken dinner for only fifteen cents.

We've come to the former site of the Elite Barber Shop,
where the Mills Brothers, Lester Granger, "Pig Meat" Mark-
ham, and other black celebrities came regularly to be "shown"
(head shaved) or "fried" (the kinks removed). The old
residents now tell you nostalgically how the traffic was tied
up for blocks, on both sides of Seventh Avenue, when Joe
Louis was in the barber's chair.

At the Red Rooster, on Seventh Avenue, I talk with the
barmaid, tall, regal Fannie Pennington. She keeps a glossy
print of her former boss, Adam Clayton Powell, smiling among
the bar bottles. Most of the other bars have pictures of the
slain Martin Luther King, between the two slain Kennedy
brothers.

Fannie mentions that I might get a room at Adam Powell's
"Guest House," adjacent to his church. Until its purchase by
the Abyssinian Baptist Church the Guest House was run by

the YWCA. The church was founded by the Reverend A. Clayton Powell, Sr., father of the Congressman, and one of the community's best-known religious leaders at the turn of the century.

With the intention of calling the Guest House, I hobble to the back of the place to use a pay phone. The phone rings and automatically I answer. A male voice asks for a Dr. Grant. Momentarily disconcerted, I explain this is a bar, that I'd just been passing by; then I shuffle back to check with Fannie. As luck would have it, Dr. Grant walks in.

When Dr. Grant, in his forties, slightly built, with jet-black skin and a kindly expression, returns from the phone booth, I am seated at a table close enough to hear him talk with his friends at a round table. While Dr. Grant and his friends (one girl resembles Dolores del Rio) finish a round of drinks, I learn that the doctor has his offices above the Red Rooster.

Gradually I move in on his circle, listening. After the second round of drinks Dr. Grant perceives my intention of capturing his attention (I plan to present him with my feet) and he invites me to take an empty chair at the same table. I move over and meet the beautiful girl, Connie Wright, and the others. Dr. Grant tells me he has three clinics, where he dispenses methadone, a synthetic drug which, taken with an orange-drink powder mixed with water, eliminates an addict's craving for dope. "The orange mix costs about five cents per serving and the methadone even less," Dr. Grant said.

Connie Wright suggests that by putting the addicts on methadone, "You are just substituting one form of addiction for another."

"In one sense you are right," he replies, but then he adds that unlike most serious addicts, the men using the methadone are able to live normal lives. "One of my patients is getting his degree in electronics this year at Columbia. Others go regularly to a job every day. They feel no compulsion to have the drugs. They can lead normal lives."

I wait until the doctor finishes a martini before asking if he'd mind looking at my feet. He has already closed his offices upstairs—he is getting ready to leave for a vacation—but he says he'll reopen his clinic. He takes me into an examination room, props my feet up, opens one large blister—and white liquid pours as from an open faucet. He says what I am beginning to realize: that infection is the great danger and that if I am not careful I might lose entire toes—and even my feet.

"I'd want to give you penicillin before opening all those other blisters, especially those around the toes," he said. He asked if there was any reason why I couldn't take penicillin. I knew I shouldn't take it without first checking with either Dr. Lerner in New Haven or Dr. Kenney in Washington, who gave me the pills to change my color.

What should I tell Dr. Grant? He was a man who had closed his office, was relaxing before leaving on vacation. He had opened his clinic and was doing all this to be helpful to me, was doing it out of the goodness of his heart, as a friend. With him it would be silly to be coy and evasive. I knew I could not lie to him.

"I've been taking another medication. The doctor said for me not to take anything else without first checking."

"What is the medication?"

"Psoralen."

"I've never heard of it." Then, "Why are you taking it?"

"Because . . . because . . . to make my skin black."

The doctor looked up sharply, as if seeing me for the first time—or, perhaps, trying to see me anew, and then, still with surprise, "—well, what are you, are you a white woman?"

I said, "What do you think?"

"To tell the truth I hadn't thought of it one way or the other. I had seen you only as a human being."

Dr. Grant and I agree that before he gives me penicillin I should check with either Dr. Lerner or Dr. Kenney. "I'll put on some clean bandages," he said. "And we'll hope for the best." Since he was leaving town he gave me the name of another Harlem doctor, Thomas Day, whom I can call in case of an emergency.

The next morning, and still at the Douglas Hotel. I look at my feet, and I summon the strength from somewhere outside myself to keep moving them.

I came here with only twenty dollars in my purse so that the financial strain (and this no doubt is feminine "logic") would appear more difficult than the physical or psychological.

Now I must get to a bank. I have money in a Washington bank that I want to transfer by check to a Harlem bank.

I move down the street, amid the garbage cans piled higher and higher. Why, why isn't it ever collected? But in Harlem one only gets the questions; there are no answers. Now my lungs fill up with the putrid air, and I see the weaving addict, the mother coming from the dirty stoop. "Hey!" the woman shouts to an eight- or nine-year-old boy, out on the streets, out of school, "go to Sam's and get me a 'Bud.'" It's not even nine in the morning; this is her breakfast?

The people smile, say a "Good morning," and when I talk to the women they call me "dear," "sweetheart," or "honey."

These sudden kindnesses are the wheels that keep the ghetto moving. All ghetto residents are dressed up with no place to go. But without exception they are kind to me. Good God! Negroes were never kind to me, they always looked dour, sullen, like they didn't trust me. Now it's different. They understand me, they are my fellow sufferers. We recognize that the ghetto is hell but that we're in it together. And the spirit is plain: for four hundred years we've smiled, licked boots, played prostitute, told the lies the white man wanted to hear. We put our best selves forward, giving the white man not only our physical energies as field and house slaves, but our best music and religious devotion. Now it's time for us to help ourselves, us niggers.

I wander into Teddy's Shanty to get some breakfast. A rotund white man with cigar sits in a corner, watching a Negro waitress check the silver. So, he can't trust the help. His briefcase is on the counter and I feel sure he owns Teddy's. I watch the young black dandies come and go. They don't own anything in Harlem, just their skintight trousers, with fine suede jackets costing $100 or $150 each. Sociologists call this "compensatory consumption," which I take as a fancy term to mean the poor blacks don't own the business, they merely own nice clothes.

A waiter comes to take my order. "Do you have any grits?" "No," he says. He and I are in each other's eyes, soul all the way. He has no compunction about recommending a competitor. "Why don't you go across to Whimpies? They have grits."

I take his suggestion, and after the grits, and bacon, I walk to the Chase Manhattan Bank, across from Harlem Hospital emergency ward. Inside I find a replica of white American efficiency; four sky-blue-and-gray steel desks are perfectly spaced, and behind them sit four white executives looking as confident as if they'd been placed on top of the world and told to run all the land, seas, cities, and people below.

Encouraged by his smile, I approach one of the executives and sit in a vacant chair before him. Benevolently he asks what he might do to help me, and I blurt out too loudly (because the place has a sanctified air): "Can you tell me where I can find a *black* bank?"

"A what?" and he shouts louder than I had blurted, so that others who had been quietly transacting their business now turn to see the commotion. He lowers his voice: "A *what* did you say?"

"You know," I tell him, "a bank black people own, a bank where Negroes control the capital. I don't have anything against *your* bank," I hasten to assure him. "I know it's a fine, reliable bank, but I live in Harlem and want to do business with a black bank."

"No, I don't know." He says it firmly, and is standing, indicating that I, too, should be on my feet. Somewhat urgently he motions for the next visitor to move in and for me to move out. Spurned, feeling insipid, I slink toward the door when a black man on the other side of the bank lobby motions me to his side. He is a bearded man, with briefcase in hand, and he waits until I get almost inches from his face before he speaks. I realize he is *whispering*. He gives directions ("Walk a couple of blocks, get off the bus on 125th, walk over to Eighth") that are simple enough, but his furtive, nervous glances and low, confidential whispers indicate we are engaged in espionage.

On a bus, engrossed in my own thoughts, I become aware that I have begun to see beyond the *blackness* of Harlem. A black among blacks, I have forgotten to "see" black so much as people, individuals: fat, short, clean, dirty, pretty, ugly. In this way, I now glance around me, vaguely noticing my fellow passengers. One is a young man, perhaps twenty-two, who has boarded the bus just behind me.

He has a can with newspaper wrapped around it. The can catches my attention because its wrapping is so neat, almost as if someone did nothing but wrap cans with newspaper all day. As soon as the young man sits down and the bus is rolling, he brings the can to his lips and drinks from it. Only moments later he is in a stupor, nodding, and no longer in control of his head, which falls to one side. What had been in the can? What pills had he swallowed before he drank from the can? It is useless to imagine. Dope is now so prevalent in Harlem that the varieties and ways of taking it are as numerous as the addicts.

We passengers seem all to have been aware of the young man leaving our world, the reality of a midmorning bus ride in the heart of the ghetto. Seeing him depart from us, we feel the unity of sorrow-pain.

None of us on the bus stares at the young man, no one by voice or glance gives judgment, yet no one looks away. This scene is an every-day-of-the-week scene in Harlem, and no one can look away.

I get off the bus at 125th Street and locate the Freedom National Bank. I ask a black official seated behind a desk plate with the name C. C. Norman on it: "Is this a black-owned bank?"

"I think the majority of capital probably is black," he replies.

I like his honesty, his face, and his accent. "Are you from Jamaica?" I ask.

"I'm from Africa!" he replies, and I am impressed, not by his origins but by his being so proud of them.

"My country is Sierra Leone," he says. I search my brain for the capital of his country, so I can say something knowledgeable, but drawing a blank, I leave a $200 check for deposit, with a "Thank you, Mr. Norman." And he promptly says, "And *we* thank you, Miss Halsell."

At the Adam Powell Guest House I write out a check for a desk clerk. She is a flaccid-faced woman named "Mrs. Thomas." She eyes it suspiciously, then: "How much money do you have on deposit?" My check is for $13.50, the weekly rate.

I am so stunned by Mrs. Thomas' brazen inquiry about my bank balance that I don't even answer her. She continues to toy with the check. "And we do like for you to join the church," she says. Naturally the church is Adam Clayton Powell's Abyssinian Baptist Church, just next door. I say I can hardly wait, and in truth I would agree to go three times a day if that's what it takes to escape the dark, miserable hotel room where I have slept four nights and where I was always imagining rape or some nameless "fate worse than death."

She finally indicates I have passed her security check but by then I am so exhausted that I am forced to sit down in the nearest empty chair in the lounge. My room would be on the sixth floor. The elevator isn't working, and I have to rest before mounting all those stairs. I look around me. It is now evening. Here "at home" in the downstairs lobby are my fellow women of the Guest House.

As a black woman seated among black women, clustered around a TV set, it strikes me as strange, even idiotic, that all thoughts emanating from the screen are white-oriented, as if all the other people, the people who don't have white skin, are not really out there in the audience. One white woman on the screen claims that if she had her life to live over again, she'd live it as a blonde; and then she asks, "Wouldn't you really rather be blonde?" Looking around me I see that even tons of Clairol wouldn't do the trick for our particular gathering.

Finally I walk the six floors to the box that is my room. Seeing it, I feel wearily that with handles on it, the room could be a coffin. Nonetheless it seems a haven, a safe shore. I collapse on the bed, fall into a fitful sleep, only to be awakened by sharp, pained cries coming from my feet. I inspect them carefully, deciding that they have become infected. Positive thinking is now not only insufficient, it is naïve. I need a doctor, and quick.

In the beginning I had not realized that my malady might be connected with the medication I'd taken to turn my skin black. Now I don't know what I think, except that like a Christian Scientist, I am trying to keep "the good thought" so that the ugliness and the pain will miraculously go away.

I call for Dr. Grant. He is still on vacation. Next I try to reach the man he recommended, Dr. Day, but get an answering service, the kind that always leaves me wondering whether I'm talking to a person or machine. To make "it" realize I consider my case an emergency, I say "If I can't see Dr. Day *tonight*, I must fly to Washington to see a doctor there." The woman at the service must be human, almost. She giggles, reminding me that is "quite a distance" just to see a doctor.

Then I do what I should have done earlier. I telephone Dr. Kenney in Washington. "Doctor, I've got real bad feet."

"Don't fool around with this a minute," he says. "You might have a serious infection. And you could lose your feet!" He directs me to get the first available airplane back to Washington. He will come to my apartment.

Roscoe Dixon, whom I also call, meets me at the airport late at night. He practically carries me, through a back entrance of the Calvert, up a freight elevator, into my apartment. Dr. Kenney arrives and begins special treatments to save my feet.

He informs me that I have suffered third-degree burns on my feet from too much sun exposure in Puerto Rico. The medication I have taken to turn my skin black permits sun rays to penetrate the skin many times faster and stronger than is usual. Strangely the burns did not surface until several days after my return from Puerto Rico. I do not understand the reason for this and neither does Dr. Kenney.

"Do you have any idea," he asks, "why these severe burns are in your feet? I'm puzzled as to why the burns would be there instead of elsewhere. The skin in the feet usually is the toughest."

"You mean they could have been anyplace?" I ask, "like my

face?" Yes, he says, adding that if I wanted to do so, I could consider myself very lucky.

I do consider myself lucky.

I am bedridden for ten days. Then the doctor tells me he thinks my feet will be all right.

I am going back to Harlem. I feel like I did when as a child a horse threw me. Grounded I knew I must get back in the saddle as soon as possible, to start over, finish the job. Going back to Harlem now will be easier than going the first time, weighted down with all my fears. I still worry about my feet, and I pamper myself to the extent of flying back to New York and hailing a taxi, even though I am aware of a cynical definition of Harlem—a "place where white cabdrivers refuse to go."

We are off and running before I give the address to the driver—named Smith and colored white—or what the blacks would call a *gray*. When I casually say, "179 West 137th Street" I feign calmness, and gaze deliberately at the passing scenery. Even so I sense his staring furiously at me through his rear-view mirror. In my nervousness it seems to me he is practically careening off the highway, possibly trying to decide whether to keep going or to stop and dump me and my suitcase into the nearest ditch, or the cemetery we are approaching.

"Did you say *West* 137th?" he exclaims. "You know that's Harlem!" and then tells me what I already knew, that if I had told him the address in the first place he wouldn't have accepted the fare. "I never go there!" he says, his rage building. He is so angry that as we turn onto 125th Street he grows more and more accident prone, cursing every black driver that we pass.

How ironic, I tell myself, to meet death in Harlem, at the

hands of a white cabdriver hellbent on fleeing the hated area. I literally expect to see foam issue from his mouth as he makes first one and then another wrong turn. The meter is soaring, and we could have arrived at the Adam Powell Guest House long since had be been able to use his brains instead of his elbow. Finally, after we have circled once too often, I demand, "Let me out—*right here!*" He grinds to a halt in the middle of a block, I hand him five dollars, scamper out, take my change—and then, still living dangerously, do not tip him.

"Hey! Stupid! What y'gonna give me for driving you here?" he yells. As I struggle to move my gear to the sidewalk he continues his tirade. "Ask me to drive ya to this hell-hole, don't give me nuthin'—you stupid *black bitch!*" He hurls further profanities. I listen also to the silence of the black people, sitting on the stoops, standing in clusters. It is early afternoon, hot and sticky.

A Negro woman on a stoop calls to some children across the street, "Come help this lady." A sweet-faced boy of nine and two girls about thirteen and eleven help me get to the Guest House.

Trudging up the street with my children-helpers, I hear a voice calling, "Are your feet any better?" I turn. It is Tony, who occasionally runs an elevator at the Guest House. Since I had been there only one day, I say, "You have a great memory."

"Never forget a face," he says. And then with laughter, "—*or feet.*"

Back to the cell, the prison inside the prison, and I look around me in that small room, four walls surrounding a bed, a dresser, with one dim light bulb dangling from the ceiling. The "poverty" of my existence is in vivid contrast to what I left behind in Washington. Missing are all the comforts, amenities of home. A view from windows to gardens, flowers, trees, birds, scampering squirrels. The brightness of books, music, paintings, soft pillows. And all those luxuries I have come to take for granted: a bathroom with shower, tub, soap, all for my personal use, and not down a long, dark corridor where I must wait in line to take my turn. Living, dining, sleeping areas; kitchen cupboards and refrigerator stocked with food. A telephone. Answering service. Television. Radio. Record player. Doorman. Messengers. All familiar smells, sounds, faces.

Now in the Guest House I am a female among females, a setting I have always found alien, depressing, unnatural. The majority are big-boned, taller, stronger than I. I move among them, checking mail at the reception desk, watching TV in the lounge, waiting my turn at the pay phone, the community toilets, and shower stalls. We are all *women*, with mysterious, unfathomable, tragic-marvelous secrets that in one sense unite us. Yet I know I will know them only in a superficial way. They have lived their lives on one planet, so to speak, and I on another.

I have heard among Harlem men that the Guest House has women who make love only with other women. Now seeing the virile women with muscles like a dockworker's I think that the "fate worse than death" would be assault by a female.

One girl, as strong as an ox and attired in skintight Levis, works for the postal service, lifting sacks of mail onto delivery trucks. She is constantly in the company of a short girl, a miss "four by four," as plump as a fat chicken.

On the street, I see the two girls walking and talking together, and a black man, attracted by the "plump chicken," winks and flirts with her. The girl in the Levis, outraged that her position as masculine protector-lover has been challenged, flies into the man's face, pummeling him with her bare fists and beating him to the ground. No one interferes with this lovers' quarrel. The man, barely able to move, gets to his feet and, holding a bleeding nose, slinks dazedly away as the crazed woman fires a barrage of profanity at him. The female "girl," having looked frightened and at the same moment pleased to be the cause of so much blood, appears willing to give herself to the victor. The battle over, she bestows a worshipful glance on her escort, inserts her left arm back into her protector's right arm, and they resume their unabashed promenade.

In this instant, I suddenly see that being a real Negro male—strong, aggressive, leading—and being a Negro female—feminine, knowing herself lovable and loving—is virtually an impossibility under the rules of white society, rules which for centuries have decreed that a black woman must work like an ox and that a black man must in all instances be submissive to the white master.

I go to a "soul food" restaurant. I do not see my usual waitress, who is about forty-five who always wears slacks. She is named Melissa but is always called "Brownie." I overhear the café owner say: "*He* must really have gotten sick, because I know that *he* would have telephoned or been here . . . and *he* has never done this before, *she* must really be sick. . . ."

Confused, I ask the owner, "Do you mean Brownie? You keep saying *he*, then *she*."

"Oh," the owner explains, "*he* is both. . . ." And he says it as lightly as he would say, "Oh her name is Melissa but she likes to be called Brownie," without any judgment on his part, but only that the decision is hers and not to be questioned by him or anyone else.

The next morning drinking my coffee, I see a "man" come in for breakfast. He orders eggs, bacon, and grits and then jumps from his counter stool: "Oh, I forgot my pill!" he calls to a waitress. "I'll be right back!" He lives in the next-door apartment building and is taking pills, I am told, to grow breasts like a woman.

Later he comes in dressed in women's clothes, with an open neckline that shows his bust. Men sitting on the counter stools flirt with him, attempting, in a good-natured, mocking way to make dates. "Oh, if I can't eat without all this fuss!" he pouts. Vexed or pretending to be, he abandons his plate of food, goes to his apartment, and returns without his wig and dress, looking somewhat like a man. Only then is he permitted to eat in peace.

In telling about the Negro woman who bloodied the nose of her male rival, and the Negro man who wanted to grow female breasts, I don't want to leave the impression that I think there are more homosexuals and lesbians in Harlem than elsewhere. I don't think so. I have no comparative statistics, nor am I interested in studying any if there are such.

What does impress me is the desperate attempt of the people to break from white bondage, to "find" themselves in the history of mankind. I feel as I did when the earth was crumbling beneath me in Japan, and again in Peru, that I can literally feel the trembling of the thousands of hearts around me—the excitement, the ferment. Life, we know, is but a *search* for life, and in Harlem the search may be made desperate and even evil (by the evil of the past, the white man's evil) but nevertheless the search is real, alive, vital, vibrant.

Saturday morning: I sit alone in my coffin-room. Marcela, the diminutive cleanup woman, also a man's tailor and a professional singer, knocks, comes in to talk. We talk of being women. "Sex is not so important to a woman," she says. "It is to a man, but a woman wants only to be admired, this is what really makes a woman happy, to be told she looks nice. But we can go months and months without the sex, that's no bother.

"Women always are talking about how they carry the seed

for the babies. They don't at all. It is the man who carries the baby, it is his sperm. The woman is just the fertile soil."

But "American women," she points out, "women like you and me get to be independent, and the man wants to be the boss.

"And it's right for the man to be the boss," she says. But then she adds that she never plans to be married again. "Why should I?" she says, expecting no answer.

She has come for the sheets from my bed. I have already folded them and have them ready, inside the pillowcase. "But if a woman doesn't use her body it dries up," she goes on, "you get to be like a virgin. . . ." She tells me that she hasn't had a relationship for months and when she last did it was dry, painful. She asked a doctor and he explained that she had gotten like a virgin. But she doesn't worry. "I don't need that. . . . Lots of things to be doing." She has become a mother to thirty-nine foster children, she announces casually.

Our philosophical "soul sister" talk aside, I tell Marcela I have been surprised to find so many hangers in my closet. "There must be two hundred of them," I say. "I've never seen so many."

"Well," she says, "you know how the young girls like to buy clothes!" I have only three changes, but most of the girls and women here at the Guest House have so many clothes they can't get them all in their closets. Enormous amounts are spent on new clothes and on dry-cleaning bills. People here are always carrying clothes in cellophane wrappings, clothes they've just picked up from the cleaners.

I am getting to know the girls who live around me. My next-door neighbor, Delia, is twenty-five, with a figure like an inverted Coke bottle. It was Delia who helped me get from my sixth-floor room to the ground floor and into a taxi for my flight back to Washington when my feet were so bad I could not walk alone. I had little money on hand, and no chance to cash a check. Delia borrowed money from her best friend, a large-boned masculine girl named Sadie, who also lives down the hall. "Take it," Delia had insisted, adding, "honey, we all got to help each other in this world."

Delia is presently out of a job. Formerly she had been the only Negro waitress among white waitresses in a downtown bar that catered to wealthy playboys. She made $200 a week, had a Lenox Terrace apartment, and a Negro musician boyfriend who worked irregularly. "He objected to the bunny costume I had to wear at work," Delia told me. They had an argument and he said either the job or him, and she quit the job. Then she lost her nice apartment, they continued their quarrels, and eventually she lost the boyfriend.

Sunday afternoon. I walk into the Guest House. One of Delia's boyfriends has been to the desk and left a package for her. "Will you take this up to Delia?" the clerk asks. I tap on her door. Not getting a response I open the door, intending to leave the package. Delia is in the small bed with Sadie, oblivious to intrusions. They are making love. I quickly shut the door. Stunned, I hurry to my room, then down the flight of stairs, out onto the streets to sort out my thoughts. Delia has boyfriends. Sadie has a husband stationed in Germany. I recall having asked Sadie why she had not gone overseas with her husband. She had shrugged her shoulders, "Too much competition."

"You mean German women?" I asked.

"Yes," she replied, adding, "and the bastard loves those pale, blonde bitches."

Now it all seems hopelessly tangled.

Sunday evening: I am back in my room. Below, from the Adam Clayton Powell church, come the voices of the older generation, the ones who have had nothing in this life but hardships, and have lived through them all with the syrupy hope of the sweet bye and bye.

Sweet hour of prayer
Sweet hour of prayer
That bids me from a world of care . . .

float their plaintive voices. But the young people want it now, on this earth, not in the afterlife. They are out in the streets, they are in their tight pants and suede jackets and they are bitter about all the old lies.

Hearing the call to worship, I decide to walk around the corner to Adam Powell's church. I am in flat shoes, skirt, and blouse, with a black kerchief tied over my head. On the street a man follows me.

"Will you talk to me?" He is a tall man in a kelly-green suit, and is either high on marijuana or drunk on liquor.

"No, no, I'm on my way to church."

He keeps following me and as we turn the corner of 138th he calls, "If you won't talk to me . . . will you *make a prayer* for me?"

Yes, brother, I tell him.

Inside the church, waiting for the service to begin, I study what the women are wearing. Giving all my attention to the hats, some tall, others wide-brimmed, made of felt, velvet, feathers, I forget to say a prayer for the "soul brother" I just left on the street.

We sing the old hymns that were as much a part of my growing-up diet as cornbread and clabber. The Scripture is from Paul to the Corinthians: love suffers long, is kind; does not envy, does not behave unseemly, does not seek its own satisfaction, is not easily provoked, does not think evil. I sit there thinking evil thoughts about the tall young preacher in a $200 suit—the price tag all but glowing from the material—while he talks about not letting "seas" divide groups of people. (Powell has crossed the sea to Bimini, his Caribbean retreat, this Sunday.) We are out of the church by 7:40 P.M.

Over at the Sugar Bowl, where I stop for supper, I see two of the good sisters and comment, "It sure was short." "*Things* have gotten so bad around here," one says, "no one wants to be out late."

The following Sunday morning: I go to services at the Convent Avenue Baptist Church. One prayer, lasting thirty minutes, must have evolved from old "praise nights" back in slavery days which provided about the only chance for the Negro to express himself as freely and emotionally as possible. Adhering to the old African dictum, "the spirit will not descend without song," we sing a half-dozen songs, including selections by two choirs and a baritone solo.

And then the fantastically rhythmical sermon, with the audience as much a part of the animated narrative as the minister. Their timing is so perfect, first one, then another supporting one another, that it seems they've rehearsed it. The moral of the story is that if you get yourself in a tight place He will help you—just "call."

Preacher: "I'm gonna call up some *witnesses*."

Response: "Put them on the stand!"

Preacher: "The Lord will hear you."

Response: "Call Him up! Call Him up!"

Preacher: "There's no switchboard up there, no zip code, you can call direct—"

Response: "You got a *direct* line!"

Preacher: "He will hear you, *He* will hear you. You tell Him anything—and He doesn't go around gossiping, telling others what you told Him. . . ."

Response: "That's right, that's right. . . ."

Wednesday afternoon: Connie Wright, whom I met through Dr. Grant, tells me her favorite beautician is Wilbert Simmons who has his shop upstairs at 125th and Fifth. I make it up the steep flight of steps, ring a bell, and one of the clients opens the locked door. In a way it is like going to a tea party with a group of talkative, gossipy women. It always provides an atmosphere as intimate and cozy as a gathering of old friends. Undernourished green plants struggle against dirty window blinds, and cases of empty Coke bottles are arrayed against a wall where a neglected calendar shows us December three years past.

The TV set sobs out the interminable love triangle of the daytime serial. And we are all soul sisters with Wilbert, our soul brother, who like God has heard all about the most secret chambers of a woman's heart.

Shampooing my hair, Wilbert works in a strange liquid. "What's that?" I ask, frightened that in his assembly-line production he might "process" my hair.

"Never mind," he replies. "You don't walk out of *here* with just a plain shampoo like you would at Macy's or Gimbels." Like any expert operator in Tokyo, Cairo, or Chihuahua, Wilbert rolls my hair in about eight minutes. Other customers study "hair style" magazines as they would a text. The models pictured are white, with soft, silky hair. In slavish imitation the black women suffer the tortures of hell to turn their kinks into what they themselves always refer to as "good" (straight) hair.

From the conversation swirling about me, I learn that the Negro women get their hair "pressed" about once a week. The hair may be chemically straightened with alkaline that is rinsed out with water afterward; or, acid may be used, and this is like a permanent in reverse.

A teen-ager who has come in with her grandmother is ready for the dryer.

"What you gonna have?" the girl asks the grandmother, who replies, "I'm going Afro."

"What will Grandpa say?" the girl asks, covering her face with her hands in mock alarm.

The grandmother goes over to Wilbert's chair, and he puts the irons on the fire to heat. So, it was a joke. She would not go Afro. Presently Wilbert runs the hot irons through her hair, then applies a hot comb to straighten the hair. The once kinky hair now stands straight out, like sheets in the wind. Wilbert, sniffing all the burned hair, complains that he can't stand the smell, and throws open a window.

As I come out from under the dryer I hear a Mrs. Jones, a retired schoolteacher, talk about the New York City school strike, and how the Negroes in some city school districts are "bowing to the whites." She says, "We've no one to blame but ourselves . . ." and that the whites ("they") always seek out any intelligent Negro and put him or her in a prestige position, where they are certain the Negro will remain silent. "They put the outstanding Negro teachers into some job with a title but no effectiveness. Look at Thurgood Marshall, he was a good lawyer, we needed him. Now he's on the Supreme Court, but he can't help. And Senator Brooke, nothing but another Uncle Tom. And Jackie Robinson—moving among the whites, working for Governor Rockefeller. He could have come back here and taught others what he had learned. But he's forgotten Harlem."

Mrs. Jones says that "even if Negroes like Robinson and Brooke try to live exactly like the whites, *they* will still treat you like a Negro, even if you've got 1 per cent Negro blood. . . ." And she adds, "*You* know what I mean, *you* understand." She says some of the "well-off" lighter-skinned Negro people refuse to send their children to Harlem schools, and she repeats, talking directly to me, "We've no one to blame but ourselves."

I am ready to leave, but a sudden rain shower delays me. I sit down to wait, and listen to Mrs. Jones:

"I see these young girls going around exposing all of their bodies. I'm on the streets every day, I see it all, but I will never deny them, *my* people. No, no. I am one of those who hasn't run away. . . . I can't."

The TV blasts away, the girls keep talking. Among them is a skyscraper Jane in Levis, who drives the ninety miles from Poughkeepsie each week to have her hair done. I glance at the three women who are getting their hair straightened, sitting in various stages of the processing. Wilbert goes first to one, then the other, rubbing white foamy goo into their hair.

I feel sure Wilbert has his own formula, but I had read that when he was a boy Malcolm X had made his own, slicing up a couple of white potatoes in a fruit jar, adding some Red Devil lye, two eggs, stirring real fast—and producing a pale-yellowish jellylike mixture known as congolene. First his friend massaged in vaseline, then combed in the congolene—like raking off the skin, or hell-fire-and-damnation—and then soap-lathered the head, to put out the fire.

Malcolm later said, "How ridiculous I was! This was my first really big step toward self-degradation: when I endured all of that pain, literally burning my flesh to have it look like a white man's hair. I had joined the multitude of Negro men and women in America who are brainwashed into believing that the black people are 'inferior'—and white people 'superior' —that they will even violate and mutilate their God-created bodies to try to look 'pretty' by white standards."

Now, at Wilbert's, noting the press of business, I comment: "Wilbert, you're so busy, maybe I could help around here."

"Are you crazy?" he responds. "Just what I need, a helper without a license! They'd close me down in a day. Besides," he adds, "my customers don't let nobody touch their hair 'cept me. You know Ella Lee, the opera singer? She's from Texas, like you. She will fly here from anyplace, like—all the way from Spain—just to get me to do her hair."

I knew, from reading such magazines as *Ebony*, which features in each issue many full-page ads for hair straighteners, that black women devote a large part of their time and energy to a woman's "crowning glory," her hair.

In my walks I have seen two and three beauty shops to every block. Many stay open twelve to fifteen hours a day. Some shops are open when I go out at 7 A.M., and some still are open at 10 or 11 at night. Some are privately operated and hire assistants; others have managers and rent out booths to individual operators for eighteen to twenty dollars a week. Prices are about the same as the white-owned shops. I paid Wilbert five dollars for a shampoo and set.

On my way home from Wilbert's I stop to have coffee at Whimpies and chat with Loretta, who lives down the hall from me and who notices my hair has just been done. She suggests that next time I should go upstairs to the Apex Beauty School, where she has just had her hair "straightened." "They like customers, that's part of their training," she tells me, "and you get your hair done for half the price. Go in some morning, but not before ten—they first have religious services."

"Religious?" I ask.

Yes, she explains, the school is run by a church group that insists the students all sing a song and say prayers before they get started with the hot irons.

Loretta leaves. I linger over my coffee and try to imagine myself in the skin of a young Negro girl wanting a career other than domestic service, to imagine that I have decided to study hair styling. I imagine I have worked as a waitress, at fifty dollars a week, saving up until I have $700 for the tuition and that I somehow manage to provide room and board for myself for the eight months while I study—eight hours a day—to get my diploma. The day arrives—today! I can do anything with hair, I am the best in the class. Ready, world!

As the black operator, I seek, knock, ask—where? At a white beauty shop? At a downtown Washington, D.C., or New York City beauty shop? If any white beauty shop in the United States hires me as an operator I'd probably be the very first one. The white shops let black women sweep the floors. They let them wash the hair—but never *set* it!

Back at the Guest House I climb the six flights to my room, then go into the community bathroom to shower—what a stifling, humid night! I try to open the one window, which is shut tight, when I hear Loretta's voice, "Don't open the window!"

"Oh, are you back ?" I ask. Then, about the window: "I just thought it was terribly hot!"

"I have an allergy. Just wait—I'll be out soon," she calls from a tub.

In the shower, I realize: of course, she knows the hot, humid air can bring back the kinks! They can pop back in at the most awkward, most unfair of all times! Even when a woman is making love, if she gets steamed up, doesn't restrain herself, then she might perspire and this can cause a beautiful processing job to go down the drain. Life *is* unfair!

Morning. I wake early, out of habit from my childhood days when I heard the roosters crowing. I'm out on the streets before seven. I go to Whimpies for breakfast.

A pale-skinned white girl, almost albino, walks in. I am startled to see a white person here. She is nineteen or twenty, with long, straight blonde hair down past her shoulders, jet-black false eyelashes, and a miniskirt that ends about where a bathing suit begins.

"Hello, *baby*," Charles, the black waiter, greets her. While Charles studies "baby" I study the brown-skinned waitress who works alongside Charles and seems to have first claim. The blonde says she'll have a large orange juice.

"Two cans of it?" Charles asks. She nods yes.

"How you liking your classes?" Charles asks when he sets the tall drink in front of her. I judge she's a schoolteacher. She smiles a tired smile, saying they are all right. "It's good to have first graders, because they're still scared, and don't give you too much trouble." Charles nods, in his empathy. "But the older ones," and she pauses, looking him in the eyes, "they can be *hell!*" The brown-skinned waitress, I note, isn't looking quite so sympathetic as Charles. The blonde finishes her drink and sort of prances out, proud of her long white legs, so much of them showing from the mini.

I see a vagrant in a back booth who looks like he has been drunk all night. Other customers near him console him occasionally. "Did you hurt yourself?" I hear one man asking, solicitously. I think here there's hardly anyone who can't understand his neighbor's hell.

A man at the counter next to me, after ordering the house specialty, waffles and fried chicken (yes, chicken for breakfast), shouts to a friend out on the sidewalk, "Hey, Bill! C'mon in here!" Bill wanders forlornly to the counter and his friend adds, "You look like you just lost your best friend!"

"Yes," mutters Bill. "The President—" *The President!* And I'm aghast until I hear Bill continue—"Abe Lincoln." After all these years, is he still the Negro's best friend?

Walking, sitting in restaurants one can study people, as I have done for the past weeks. But I need more. I need a focus, an anchor, a routine. I need to get myself off the streets, to acquire a sense of belonging. I decide to apply for a job at Harlem Hospital. On the streets, walking there, I am a black among blacks, and I feel myself most black when I see white cops cruising by. I know the tension that the black people feel when they wonder, in fear: what are *they* doing, why are they peering so closely? With these white policemen, I have none of the sense of "protection" that I would ordinarily feel. It is as if they are the natural enemy. Had I been in trouble I'm not so sure that I would not have run from the police.

In Harlem Hospital's personnel office I talk with a Mrs. Harrell. "What can you do?" she asks, and I realize that despite my having earned big salaries there aren't many jobs I can do. "Are you a nurse? A nurse's aide?"

I had wanted to work in the kitchen, or as a waitress, but I fear that my feet will not bear up under such a burdensome job. "I can type," I tell her at last.

She sends me over to a manual machine, and it is like plowing forty acres to hammer out a page on that antiquated machine.

Returning to Mrs. Harrell with my sample, I am like a schoolgirl, confessing error: "I meant to underline here, but I X'ed out that entire sentence."

She gives it a cursory glance, "Don't worry about it, honey." I take her word of endearment as I would swallow a tranquilizer. Despite the salary (about thirty-five dollars a week) I realize that I desperately want to qualify.

Mrs. Harrell hands me other forms, more questionnaires. The hum of activity is around me: clattering machines, clattering high heels, jangling telephones, men somberly quarterbacking yesterday's games, taking their coffee breaks, moving papers from "in" to "out" baskets. I glance at the cluttered desks, the coffee cups strewn on all the tables and desks, the walls with current and vintage calendars. Studying a calendar, I realize it is three years to the day since I had gone to work at the White House. And now there are so many similarities: the fingerprinting, the forms to fill out, the tedious chore of meeting people, learning where the materials are kept (envelopes here, paper there) and watching a clock that never moves. Already, five hours since I have eaten breakfast. The air inside seems stifling. I look through a dirty glass window, and beyond, to the free world.

My reverie is interrupted by Mrs. Harrell's heels. She has my résumé in hand. "Here's twenty years of your life for which you haven't accounted!" she tells me. "You have to put *something* in that space."

Twenty years! Not just two or three or four, but twenty! I have always told the truth, about my name, age, zip code, and all the rest, and my sins are those of omission rather than of commission as far as the questionnaires are concerned. I lower my head to half mast, wondering how I might account for such a large gap in my life. I need a simple explanation, one that will cover a multitude of sins and varied aspects of life that can never be neatly capsuled or fully exposed. Finally I mutter: "I was . . . married."

"Honey," she replies, "there may be some things in your life you want to forget, but just put them down—and *then* forget them!"

The next morning: I report to medical services, where a woman gives me a pink slip with directions about where to go. I walk from the main building through various corridors and hallways to the "K" building, where a woman pricks my finger, for blood. I had gone there yesterday, and the same woman had pricked my finger. "We did this yesterday," I say softly, but she isn't listening.

Back to an elevator, my finger covered with a small piece of gauze. "Sticking holes in you, already, so early in the morning?" the man operating the elevator asks. Everyone around me has something to say, some remark, to let you know that he is aware of you, that he sees you. He creates you, in his awareness of you.

Finally, Mrs. Harrell tells me she has been trying to get Mr. S., the administrator in whose outer office I will sit, typing. "But they gave a testimonial dinner for him last evening and he's not coming in . . . you know how these administrators are." I realize she is putting herself and me in a circle of the "working people" who must bear with the Mr. S.'s of this world, because she adds, "They do what they like. He won't be in today or tomorrow." She suggests that I check back with her in two or three days.

Walk with me in the streets of Harlem. We are swimming in a sea of blackness—all of the faces passing us on the street, coming and going, crossing the streets, selling us the morning paper, serving us the morning grits, bacon, and eggs, moving around us in the workaday world, waiting on us in any of the stores—all are black. Now, go with me to the cash register, wherever that may be—at the dry cleaners, in the florist's shop, in the crummy, dirty, grocery store—with the stalest of vegetables and rotting fruit—and *there* sits a *white* man.

It continues unbearably hot and steamy. I need a few cottons, nothing fancy, just something very simple, inexpensive. "Is there a Montgomery Ward in Harlem?" I ask the women at the Guest House. Or a Sears? None around, they say. That's a surprise, even *underdeveloped* countries have Sears. Well, what about Macy's, Gimbel's, or Bloomingdale's? No, not even a branch store. *Any* well-known department store that sells name brands and stands back of its "guaranteed" merchandise?

But no, there's no store one from the Outside World might have heard of, unless it is Blumstein's, a white-owned store in the heart of Harlem, where in 1957 a deranged woman, Mrs. Izola Ware Curry, stuck a Japanese letter opener into the chest of Martin Luther King, Jr., when he arrived to autograph copies of his first book.

Blumstein's, then, is in the "heart" of the shopping district, and you almost have to laugh, or maybe cry, when you call the Harlem shopping district by that name.

I walk the "main drag," the Broadway of Harlem, and it's

a short walk—there on 125th, between Eighth and Lenox. It's more like a carnival or a tent show, or let's say the Lubbock County Fair of 1936. I pass one small, trashy store after another, and the merchandise is not so much displayed as poured into windows. Inside the stores the goods are piled up on counters like giveaway stacks for the Salvation Army.

Where does all this come from? Did someone discover a stockpile of prewar made-in-Japan goods? Or some remnants from downtown fire and close-out sales? Even in Iquitos, Peru, in the heart of the biggest rain forest in the world, with no roads leading into or out of the place, I found more attractively displayed merchandise than in Harlem, U.S.A.

Before going to live in the ghetto, I, like others, had heard that the poor pay more—and get less. And you think to yourself, serves 'em right! They don't have to buy in Harlem! Why don't they study the ads for sales at Gimbel's, Macy's, Bloomingdale's, and other New York stores? They could shop at Korvette's. And there are Sears and Montgomery Ward—someplace or other. Why don't they hop on a bus or a subway or get in a car and go to these places, prowl through bargain basements, compare prices all over town? After all, poor people may live in the slums but they aren't *chained* there.

All I can say is that now that I am in the ghetto to live I feel chained here; it is unreal, and yet painfully real, too.

There are no walls in the ghetto, and this is as true as saying that if you close your eyes you cannot see anything while there is plenty you can see. The ghetto walls exist as walls, terrible as those "green curtains" that closed in on me in the jungle, sealing me off, so that I felt I could not move beyond the enclave where I and others like me were camped out. Beyond were places I should not go; *out there* in that other world lies something monstrous and menacing. They don't want you out there!

Here, I feel that if I go downtown the psychological strain of crossing over and then crossing back again will be so great that I can't manage it. I lack the will or courage to go through the invisible but nevertheless real wall that separates the ghetto from the other world.

Now walk with me. Watch the black women shop in Harlem. It is easy to see that they are not price- and quality-conscious. They do not shop; they succumb—to fast sales talk.

I'm standing in front of a store on 125th Street, trying to price a few items, when a white salesman walks outside, and starts reeling me in like a fish. "Hello *there*, my name's Steve!" —and he's smiling as though it's the beginning of a beautiful friendship. "Interested in a nice *colored* TV set today? You can try it out. *No expense. . . .*" I see myself as two persons, a reporter looking on as from a great distance, and then the other woman, the black consumer, going into a kind of trance, a dream world, yielding, uncomplaining, benumbed.

What is she dreaming? She's dreaming of the possibilities of possessions, a TV set, a watch, a ring, a hi-fi, and she imagines that these worldly goods will raise her up in the world, move her along farther toward the American dream of success—and equality. The salesman is talking to her as if they both understand what America is all about—*to get things,* that these things represent prestige, that others will then look up to her (as she has been conditioned to look up to others).

Mesmerized I listen to all the marvels of the color TV, and mutter a question about the price. Now I have said a word that does not exist in the Harlem language. There are *no* prices. The word "price" is never mentioned; it is a word Steve does not even understand. You might just as well say the word "price" in Greek or Chinese—he would not know what you were talking about (as far as you could see). It doesn't cost a *price,* it costs *one dollar down,* the rest comes on *easy* installments. And this is the way Steve and all of Harlem —or at least 90 per cent of it—operates.

On all the items in the store windows I never see a "price tag" so that I can compare the price of a TV set here with that of a TV at Macy's or one of the downtown stores. A ghetto salesman keeps a set of "numbers"—a number that for him represents a wholesale price, and then various other numbers for the customers, depending on how dumb they are.

In addition to the color TV, Steve shows me a set of dishes, and since the tag says *one dollar* (it's the same, whether it's a pair of shoes for the baby, a sewing machine, or a hi-fi) I ask about the carrying charges. I listen very carefully, but it would take two astute lawyers arguing for a week to come to an agreement, if indeed they ever could, on what Steve really says, so diverse and misleading are his explanations. I get the point: why worry about details, just pull out one measly greenback, sign "here" and the set of dishes is yours!

I see black women signing "here" without bothering to read the contract. They feel that, should it come down to contesting the contract, justice would be stacked rather heavily on the side of the merchant. So, they don't read the contract, nor do they demand a copy for themselves. They take the goods and hope for the best, and when they don't get it, they feel the utter and complete frustration that leads to throwing rocks through the window of the store.

And why, you might ask, do white merchants continue to locate in these areas? And why do they return, riot after riot? The merchants return because black people are great consumers. Slum business is profitable business. In Harlem, the rioting's end saw only the pawnshop owners put out of business, because they lost goods they could not repossess.

Thus, interminably, the white salesmen make their pitch and the black consumers cart out the merchandise, happy for the moment that the possessions will mark a *style* of life, if not life itself. The customer, having taken the goods on the installment plan, will return the following week to make a payment, and while he's in the store the salesman will persuade him to take still another item, for *"one dollar down."* The black consumer now becomes more and more beholden, setting a pattern reminiscent of the Southern sharecropper's relation to the country store.

Because Harlem lives on credit, the black consumers and the white merchants are engaged in a kind of dance of death: black people have their wants constantly stimulated by high-powered advertising and fast-talking salesmen. They have poor judgment, too little cash—and whatever their future wages, they're pledged for goods purchased in the present. They are therefore poor credit risks. The merchants then say they must place a high markup on low-quality goods to protect themselves against these poor credit risks.

Should the customer fail to make payments, the merchant can repossess the goods, but he seldom does because his merchandise is so shoddy, even when new, that it doesn't last long. The merchant can sue, and, winning a court judgment, can have the customer's property attached. Should this fail to satisfy the debt, he can have the customer's salary appropriated, or *garnisheed*—a word that everyone in Harlem knows only too well.

I have started working at Harlem Hospital. I must discipline myself to sit all day long, typing. So far it seems dull and tedious, and I realize that most people in this world are tied to jobs that they do not necessarily like. Again I think that my life has been singularly blessed, inasmuch as I have always done the kind of work I thoroughly enjoyed.

Now I will leave the Guest House and try living on my own in an apartment. I have found a place in the same building where Delia formerly lived. She has introduced me to the "super," a crippled man in his sixties. He showed me a vacant room, with a stove, refrigerator, and bath. The over-all space is about ten feet by twelve but it seems like a great luxury to me now to have a private bath, and an icebox and stove. Until now I have been dressing at six, going out for my first cup of coffee because I always want coffee when I wake up.

I've had another stroke of luck. The "super" took me to the basement and showed me a bed and chest of drawers left by the former tenants. "You can have them for fifty dollars," he said, and I readily agreed to furnish the apartment by this means. Now all I need are a few linens. The rent is ninety-five dollars a month, which is considered very cheap in Harlem. Many girls I know pay twenty-five dollars a week for a room, with no cooking facilities.

I have become very chummy with Connie Wright, the friend of Dr. Grant. She is a welfare worker and lives at the Lenox Terrace apartments. This evening we agree to meet at Jock's restaurant. A friend comes by. When Connie introduces him as Clifford Henry Jones he replies good-naturedly, "I've got just as much right to three names as Princess Margaret's husband." He sits down with us and says he's known Connie "and all her family" for years.

Connie and Cliff, as she calls him, now engage in a most intimate conversation, dealing with matters of the heart.

"I'm not living until I have an emotional commitment, how about you, Connie?" Cliff asks. She agrees. And then he asks, "How long has it been since you were all tied up with someone, *in your guts?*" And she replies, 1958. Then she asks him and he mentions a date. I am listening only in a cursory way, noticing a tall, regal black girl in a dramatic bell-bottom slack outfit and her hair *au naturel*. I am studying the girl and her escort when Cliff asks, "Is it possible for any man to talk to you *as a woman?"* I know he is somewhat annoyed that I have not given him all my attention. "You might try talking with me *as a person,"* I reply.

Now, since he has called attention to himself, I shut out some of the external distractions and look at him really for the first time. He is somewhat casually but expensively dressed. He has oblong brown eyes, flat Negroid nose, and very light skin, several shades lighter than mine. His thinning hair is cut down to the scalp and I imagine that he wears a stocking cap, literally a part of a woman's stocking, on his head at night so that his naturally fuzzy hair will stay down flat when he removes the stocking. Jones, I learn, has a $15,000-a-year job heading a neighborhood poverty program.

He talks passionately, but, I notice, with controlled emotion, of his utter sense of failure and the complete frustration he knows in dealing with the blacks. He speaks always of "them" as if he is white and not one of "them."

He talks of being "militant," but he is far from that, and is, rather, a perfect example of an "MC," as the militants term the middle-class Negro, who goes in for golf and identifies with the lost causes of thirty years ago and acts as master of ceremonies for programs whitey controls.

Now I listen to Mr. Jones: "I can't go with those Rams, or Black Panthers, they'd destroy *all.* I'm a militant, but one with a purpose. You have to have something, some reason for tearing everything down. But, I don't know the way.

"What *is* the solution? This poverty program was doomed from the beginning—the poor can't manage it. I don't blame the white people for their disgust—I've never seen such dumb bastards! They'll never get this off the ground. You might just as well have done this program like Roosevelt—dole out some money."

He speaks with horrified-pity-contempt for thirteen- and

fourteen-year-old girls, with "their skirts up to here" selling themselves on the streets, and, in some cases when they are offered job opportunities, replying, "I'm going to live with my boyfriend." In answer to "what does he do?" she replies, "He's a hustler." And what's a hustler? (He knows but he asks.) "You know, a little pot, some hashish . . . and pimping."

I keep wondering about his belligerence and disgust for the black poor.

"But if the white man controls all of the legitimate business," I ask, "what else can the black man do, except what is illegitimate?"

Jones suddenly drops the subject. He studies his watch, "Got to get home, and change," he tells us. "Some gal is waiting for me to pick her up." He asks Connie if he can drop us off anywhere, and we follow him to his late-model sports car, double-parked out front. At her Lenox Terrace apartment, Connie invites me up for a nightcap. She puts on some Frank Sinatra records and pours us both a Scotch. "Cliff and I both started school together," she tells me. "He was so handsome *all* the girls were running after him, we all thought he had *savoir faire*. I almost married him, but then he married Muriel, my best girlfriend, and later she told me some of their problems."

Cliff was young and strong and they enjoyed intercourse every night, she relates in a casual intimate manner. Sometimes he had an erection two and three times in the same night. After a few years Muriel had given birth to two children and Cliff had risen steadily in his health-welfare government job. One day Cliff was making an inspection of an antiquated Harlem building. He was alone in an elevator when the cables broke and the shaft fell downward in an abrupt, harrowing plunge that, miraculously, caused no physical injury. After a thorough examination doctors told Jones he had suffered only "severe nervous shock."

After a short interval, Cliff resumed his job and normal activities. Though his physical strength was unimpaired, he discovered he was impotent. He went to a doctor for a checkup and in the course of a thorough examination the doctor put his finger in Cliff's rectum to massage his prostate gland. This action caused sperm to flow and gave him a form of artificial satisfaction. But whom could he ask to engage in this kind of "love-making" with him, since he could not practice scx in conventional ways.

He told Muriel about his problem and she gladly complied by meeting his special needs, but Cliff was well aware that he wasn't satisfying her desires.

Both had once been passionate, natural, strong and greedy for the other. Now they both felt embarrassed, Cliff more than Muriel. He would not stop berating himself, and even went so far, in a bitter outburst, to urge Muriel to get herself "a man," naming one of their friends called Horse, who was a strong physical-fitness teacher. Perhaps it was the power of suggestion, but Muriel did go to bed with Horse and the result was as Cliff had imagined: sex had its way, with Muriel leaving Cliff and marrying Horse.

"That was a long time ago," Connie says. "I don't think Cliff has loved anyone but Muriel, and he adores his children and now his grandson. He just lives for that grandson. He still dates, and probably will be calling you. I could tell he likes you," Connie told me.

Later in the week: I'm typing at Harlem Hospital. The phone, a man's voice, "This is Clifford Henry Jones"—still using his three names. He asks me to dinner. I say fine and he picks me up at my apartment. We drive to Frank's Restaurant on 125th Street, where I know middle-class Negroes in Harlem pay big prices to be served by white waiters.

When we enter Jones takes my hand and guides me. He is showing all the clients and the waiters that he is out with a new date. He wants his "regular table," and a *maitre d'* responds, "Right this way, Mr. Jones."

A waiter takes Jones's order for drinks, and hands us menus that cover most of the table. Jones asks, "How is the roast beef?" I note the prices are about the same as if we'd been eating at the Waldorf-Astoria, and I calculate that Jones will spend about thirty dollars for this dinner for two. "You say *rare*," Jones is saying to the waiter, who is rotund and Irish, "but I want it *very rare*."

"Yes sir, yes sir, Mr. Jones," the waiter promises. My thoughts, my eyes, and my mind wander all around the restaurant. I know that for decades it has been white-owned and probably still is.

Suddenly I realize the waiter has gone and Jones is fuming: "You're not supposed to be staring out into space, at the scenery. I brought you here. How about looking at me for a change?"

I swallow his criticism as I would my saliva. God! I realize, I must care for this man, and he for me, for why else would he want to hurt me so much and why else would I feel his words hitting me like slaps across my face. How, I wonder, can a woman be a woman with him? And how, also, can he be a man without a woman, *a complete woman*, to give him all the assurance that he needs? But I'm no good at buttering up men. I have my needs: men to praise me. Tears well up in my eyes, moving the black contacts around.

Seeing that his arrows have hit home, Cliff continues his lecture: "Another thing, you told me you had made a deposit in the Freedom National Bank, and you must be making a fairly good salary at Harlem Hospital. Why haven't you bought any new clothes? That's the same dress you wore the night we met. You knew I'd take you out to a nice place. You could have dressed up. These are all my friends in here. And," he pauses, wanting to find the right motivation for me to get dolled up, "if you are going to be a 'professional'" [and by this he meant rise above the role of domestic], "then why don't you act like one, dress like one? I mean, it will help you. You want to look your best." He is pleading at this point, looking at me as if about to add: "Well, you know, it sets you apart from *them*" [those dirty, out-on-the-street niggers].

We finish the meal, and drive around, without talking much. We are united in the silence. I know that if we continue to see each other we will become bound to each other in the way most people do, by their habit of hurting each other. And we will know that the other cares by his registering of pain. Now that he has hurt me, I can no longer chatter or be gay. Cliff, on the other hand, knowing that he has the strength to hurt me, seems happier than he has been all evening.

He parks outside my apartment building, and comes with me to the door. Will he say goodnight? I am leaving it all up to him since he has been the big boss of the evening, telling me I should keep my eyes on him and telling me how to dress and act. We get to the elevator, and he is still the master and I the slave, and we ride up to my apartment, and he takes the key from me, inserts it and we walk in.

Once inside the room, which is overly intimate because of its small size, with the bed taking up most of the space, and with its woman smells and pot plants I have put in the window, Cliff suddenly changes. It is as swift and complete as if he has switched roles in a drama. He is not the strong image now but a submissive, pliant, pleading figure, anxious to get what he wants through cajolery and concession.

"I don't have any Scotch," I tell him, "but here's a bottle of French wine." I hand him the bottle and an opener, but I notice his hands are shaking so that he can hardly manage. I want to study his eyes, but don't have the nerve.

We are both curious, testing, testing, testing. I have been in my reporter's role, letting him come to the apartment. I am frankly putting him in a test tube, aware of his sexual secret, curious to know if he will approach me, asking me, the newcomer in town, to give him the satisfaction he must be hungry to have. And he? Now that the hunter has his prey at close quarters, how will he go about the kill? I am at once bemused and a trifle fearful as well of stirring emotions I might be unable to handle.

We sip the wine and I turn the subject around to his son, who is studying to be a doctor, and his grandson. "Everyone says he looks like me," Cliff says, showing me a couple of photos he keeps in his billfold. After we've drunk half the bottle Cliff says he is getting up at six the next morning to drive to New Jersey to play golf. He tells me he bets heavily on his golf game and likes to win. He pauses at the door. He isn't going to kiss or even peck me goodnight, but I put my face up to his and we go through that kind of motion that can be called a kiss, and part for the evening.

Sexual complexes aside, I am saddened by Cliff's elaborate pretensions, his great desire to impress people. It seems stuffy, silly, bourgeois. Why must he impress other Negroes? Because he's done well and wears expensive suits, must he lord it over others? Why wasn't he more natural, why hadn't he taken me to a soul food restaurant and spent five instead of thirty dollars for the meal? Why, I think, must he be *like so many white people I know*? I realize that being black and Jones he wants to keep up with the white Joneses. And what other standards does anyone, black or white, have in this country? As one of the advertising slogans urges us, if you've got it, flaunt it.

The next afternoon I go into the Macshaw bookstore at 125th and Lenox and select some LeRoi Jones and Malcolm X literature I've been wanting to read. A tall black man, about twenty-five, suddenly offers me a Lifesaver. As we chat, he tells me his name is John.

"What is your medallion?" I ask. He fingers the empty cartridge suspended on a leather necklace: "It's the symbol of the Black Panthers."

"I'd like to have one. What does it cost?" I ask.

"A dollar."

"Would you sell me yours?"

"No, but you can get one down the street at the Black Panthers' headquarters, at 122nd." Then, casually, "Do you happen to know where 'the museum' is located?"

"Yes." He suggests that if I have the time, why don't we go together.

The museum, a small one above Goldstein's liquor store at 125th and Fifth, was hailed as a great cultural achievement for Harlem, and indeed is about the only thing of its kind in the black capital. As we walk in the direction of the museum we are completely unconcerned about Black Panthers, guns, and the so-called war between the cops and the Black Panthers that the newspapers currently are bannering. Instead, we are like two kids out of school, joyous at having the kind of leisure that allows one to think he'd like to go to a museum, and then have time enough to actually go there.

As to our meeting, John observes, "This could only happen in New York!"

"Oh," I reply casually, "it could happen many different places."

Then in a marvelous exuberance of youth he spills over with his hunger for life, pouring out his hopes, his desire to travel— "to see many different places!"—and to read (he carried an armful of books); to get through college, explore, learn, make his life meaningful. He repeats several times, "There is so little time!"

At the museum, we view an artistic "electronic" display

that shows the rhythms of urban environment. We discuss colors, techniques, and how art can move into everyday life. When I remember John had said he was a Black Panther, I marvel that human beings communicate in all kinds of ways—walking along a street together, studying flashing traffic lights as "rhythms"—laughing, feeling joy, fulfilling one's needs of companionship.

As we leave the museum, I ask John how strongly he believes in "black power." He replies that "We have to believe in black power because we've lived under white power too long."

He expresses disgust for those Negroes of the older generation whose goal in life has been to turn as white as possible, to be "accepted" into the white man's society. He's come to realize that "we blacks must break our old ties of dependency on whites, develop political and economic sinews of our own."

Through John I come to understand why black militants like white liberals even less than they like Southern crackers. At least, he says, the Southern racists "call a spade a spade." He laughs about his use of "spade" for Negro. The militants delight in exposing those aspects of negritude that the middle-class Negro tries to hide.

I compared young militant John with Clifford Henry Jones, so obviously of the middle class, who had commented to me: "I thought of adopting one of those *poor* Southern boys, bringing him up here, giving him a few benefits of the city."

John, on the other hand, spoke with disgust for the middle-class Negro and the white liberals who "let their hearts bleed for the injustices of the South, but don't do anything to help the needs of the black ghetto—on their own doorstep." Middle-class Negroes, said John, seldom identify with their ghetto brethren, taking the attitude: "I may be your color, but I'm not your kind."

A few days after our going to the miniature Harlem art museum, while talking with John on the phone, I ask if he'd go with me to a Ray Charles show.

I'd always heard of the Apollo. Sammy Davis, Jr., Nancy Wilson, Diane Warwick, Eartha Kitt, *everyone* had appeared there. In response to my naïve comment to John about being in the "heart of Harlem" at the Apollo, he calmly explained that the Apollo was not owned by black people. He called the big-time entertainers and athletes mere "showcases" for the white people, who point and say, "See what the nigger can accomplish if he's only willing to work!" But own the joint, own the team, own the theater? Never.

The theater was filled to capacity. And finally Ray Charles. Soul came shining through. The all-black audience was giving to him, and he was giving of himself.

The audience—calling out his name, sometimes low, murmuring, like a Greek chorus, other times clapping, shouting—sustained him, inspired him, in almost the same degree that he sustained and inspired them.

Charles is the true artist, having come through the worst of experiences still shouting "Glory Be!" In his sadness, his blues, he plumbs the depths of his imagination, and this makes his sadness and that of his listeners pass away. "Now we gonna have some blues. . . . I tell you, you gonna feel lighter when you leave here tonight."

After the show we go to Small's Paradise for a drink, and John asks if he can come by my apartment. I register surprise because he's making it apparent he thinks we should now go to bed.

"Why not?" he replies to my astonished reaction.

"John," I begin. "We're good friends." And he says he knows that. "And I'm the age of your mother," and he says age doesn't have anything to do with it. "And I'm just not interested." And again he says, "Why not?"

My logic is not getting me anyplace. "You," I say, perhaps meaning myself more than John, "can't go around just loving everyone."

"Well," John replies, "you can try."

Suddenly I remember he's a Black Panther, and isn't he supposed to hate everyone? I laugh so heartily and contagiously over his comment about love that he joins me. At my apartment building I get by with a goodnight kiss and go to my room still amazed about what love and hate can mean in everyday relationships.

At the door I had said to John, "You don't seem to be afraid of anything."

"I haven't been afraid since I was five."

"I have. I have always been afraid," I tell him. "But I go around *acting* as if I'm not."

He says, "It's the same, isn't it?"

Now that I have been working for a couple of weeks and have a place to stay I decide to call the first man in Harlem who befriended me, who offered to help me—Longus Moore. He does not know it but he has been helping me every day that I have been in Harlem, helping me because I am aware of his friendship. One does not have to have the corporeal being present to draw strength from him.

I call Moore and he picks me up after work at the hospital. "I've been waiting to hear from you," he tells me. "I checked the Douglas Hotel and they told me you'd left. And I didn't know where to get in touch with you. I didn't even know your last name."

We are driving around Harlem in his big blue convertible, and he shows me where he lived as an orphan. "An old lady took me in, befriended me, and now she's just a stack of bones. I have her living in my house, now. I go home two or three times during the day to check on her, to make sure she hasn't died, to ask if she wants anything, and to turn her over so she doesn't have to sleep on the same side all the time."

Suddenly he asks if I need any money, and I tell him that I don't.

I see that he has that expansive personality with a woman; here, let me bow down before you, anything you want, within my power, I will give you. Moore tells me he has worked since he was ten, standing on an orange crate washing dishes in a Greek restaurant. He has based his life on the American dream of success. And he still stands by this dream. "Plenty of opportunities in this country, more now than ever before. Why don't the young people want to work?" He has never been afraid of working: "Held three, four, five jobs at a time. I've made plenty of money. One time I had a shoe box with $30,000 in cash, and I took that shoe box into a bank. I'm not bragging, I'm just saying that I've worked hard, that others can do it, and for them, today, it would be easier than it was for me."

Then he studies me. "But you don't have to work so hard. You have to be careful, about your feet. I want . . . I want. . . ." What is he going to demand of me, what does he want of me? I clutch my hands in a vise, waiting, when I hear him telling me that he *wants to take care of me.*

"But you don't know anything about me."

"That's not important," he replies. "I don't care what you've done." Then, "You know that sign of Uncle Sam recruiting, pointing his finger, 'I want you.' Well, that's what I'm saying. 'I want you.' I don't want you just to go to bed with me. I want you, all of you, and I want to marry you, to take care of you. I've worked, and for what? I have never found the right woman for me, until I met you, and I can't explain it."

I keep wondering what replies I can make, knowing that

there is so little of myself I can give—my body or my attempt at honesty, but not all the way, and not marriage that he is suggesting. Can I explain the *why* to him? How can I be honest with Moore?

I tell him that I felt in great need when I first arrived in Harlem, that I knew no one, was frightened, and could never forget his act of friendship, and that he had framed his offer of money and help in a way that I could believe, in a way that made me feel proud to be a human being, and not in any way degraded.

But, I add, I am trying to write, trying to explore on my own, and am not that average woman who wants a man to take care of her, pay her rent, and buy her food and clothing. And I tell him that I am not what I seem, that I am not a black woman, but that I have taken pills to turn my skin temporarily black. That I am trying to find out how black people live in Harlem.

If Moore is shocked, angered, pleased, or disappointed he conceals it. Perhaps he is so accustomed to deceptions of a thousand kinds that no single one makes an impact. Perhaps, and I think this to be the case, the color of my skin, although he had admired it, was no more important to him than the color of my eyes or hair. In any case, he shrugs as if to say, "So what? Those things don't matter." But he says nothing.

I ask, "Will you let me tell about you, in the book?"

He smiles, as if to say "Why do you ask such questions, when you know the answer is yes to whatever you might want."

At first, coming to Harlem I knew a fear of the marauder, the black devil who might grab me, assault me, kill me. Now I know a new fear, the fear of not living up to Moore's sincerity. As I leave him and go to my room I wonder how in the end I can leave him without hurting him.

"You'll go away and forget me," he had said during our talk.

"No," I promised, "I won't forget you." But then I asked why he had made himself so vulnerable. "Don't you know that I could hurt you?"

"That's the way I play the game," he had replied.

The next evening Longus Moore suggests I meet him for supper at his restaurant, the Hide-A-Way, before going to a movie. At the café I study a menu of "soul food." This is the food I'd eaten all my growing-up years. It is nothing novel or strange to me, and certainly not the exclusive fare of blacks. One can say it is Southern, fried, and fattening.

In Harlem soul food includes all the simple, filling, *cheap* parts of the hog (feet, snout, tail, intestines, stomach) as well as such nourishing vegetables as black-eyed peas, okra, and collard, turnip, kale, and mustard greens. Negroes speak of "good, filling grease," a reference to their style of deep-fat frying (fried chicken, fried porgies and other fish, and hush-puppies, crusty cornmeal bread cooked in grease), which came to us from Africa, via the West Indies.

Southerners, and soul brothers and sisters, all have a big craving for sweets. Desserts at the Hide-A-Way include homemade chocolate, banana, and pineapple cakes and homemade pecan, apple, and sweet-potato pies.

The Hide-A-Way's most popular main dishes include smothered pork chops with "sweets" (sweet potatoes), barbecued ribs with a spicy red sauce, and smothered steak with mashed potatoes and white biscuits. I choose the smothered steak with collard greens and cornbread, and Moore has the smothered steak with mashed potatoes and biscuits.

After supper, we drive to see the marquees at the Roosevelt on Seventh and to Loew's on 125th. Both have grade-C horror films that even a late, late TV show would reject. I want to go to the Apollo and watch live entertainers, but Moore dismisses it as "one of the worst fire traps in New York."

"Aren't there other movie houses in Harlem?" I ask.

"No," he tells me, "they've all been sold, to be turned into churches."

"Churches! Why churches?"

"Well, what else could they turn into?" Moore replies. "Who else could be able to buy them? Nobody, except somebody who has gotten money the way the people get it from churches. The church people, the preachers, and the crooks or whoever you may call them—there's no difference, you know—they are the ones who would be in a position to extend their holdings."

Greater Harlem, Longus says, reaches below 110th Street and up into the Washington Heights area and almost from the East River to the Hudson. About one million people live here. But what recreational or cultural facilities do they have? As we drive up one street and then down another I realize why it is that as an *inmate* of this Harlem-prison one can so easily turn to prostitution, dope, or drink. There's literally almost nothing else to do! Bars open around eight in the mornings, are not required to sell food, just liquor, and by a "four for one" system can keep the black man of Harlem in a continuous stupor.

I ask Moore to take me into one of the bars. We occupy two stools, and he orders: "Scotch, please." The bartender gives him not just *one* drink but places one, two, three, *four* glasses with Scotch before him. These "four for one" drinks sell at the price of a single drink, ninety cents.

Are the owners of these "four for one" bars tampering with the liquor? Putting chemicals or artificial additives in the bourbon and Scotch to stretch it out? And if so isn't this against the law?

"Yes, there are laws," Longus says, "but they don't ever seem to catch the white man, because it's a white man who comes to inspect the place. If a colored man owns a bar and meddles with the booze, he gets caught. And then he has no more license. And it's not worth it, so he doesn't take the chance. No Negro bar owner sells the 'four for one' drinks. He knows he'll be caught."

Having nothing better to do, we decided to drive around and count liquor stores and bars. We chose the area from 155th to 110th Streets for our survey:

Lenox	Avenue: liquor stores, 17;	bars, 31
Eighth	Avenue: liquor stores, 24;	bars, 44
Seventh	Avenue: liquor stores, 18;	bars, 50
	Total 59	125

Of the fifty-nine liquor stores, "Not more than a dozen, two dozen at the most are black-owned," he says. And the bars? "The colored people own Lundy's, Linnettes, the Blue Box. . . . There may be others, but not too many more."

We pass a variety of stores: furniture, appliances, groceries, shoe shops, dry goods stores. "Practically all are white-owned," Longus tells me. "Even if you see colored workers in there, they are white-owned."

"What if they have 'soul brother' written on the outside?"

"Sometimes the soul brother might be there and he's trying to help the white man," he explains. "There used to be a store here on 125th, near Lenox, called 'Jackie Robinson's store,' and they had hundred-dollar hats in the windows, but then the colored people found out that he was fronting for the whites and they broke into the windows and they were taking the hats out and everything else. And the store did *not* belong to him. And that bar that you saw there on Seventh Avenue, called 'Count Basie'? Count Basie never had anything to do with it."

Longus explains that there aren't more Negroes in business for themselves because they can't get their hands on risk capital. In his own case he was making three dollars a week washing dishes when he won $600 at the numbers game.

On his salary, he asks, how could he ever have *saved* enough to have gone into business?

I ask if he knows of *any* black person who owns an entire building.

"A house? There's a lot of colored people who own a home on St. Nicholas Avenue, but it's not like a building, an apartment house with elevators in it. No, there's hardly any Negroes who own apartment houses. Most rent rooms, apartments. And they rent space for bars and restaurants." One exception, he says, is a Negro named Sherman who started "Sherman's Bar-B-Q," selling nothing but ribs, chicken, and pigs' feet. "There's three of 'em, and he owns his places, and he has made lots of money. But he's one of the few."

I sit typing at Harlem Hospital. I now see my job as the worst of all possible jobs for my purposes of trying to get an idea of how the mass of black people live. The people with whom I work are good top-level, intelligent, upper-middle-class people, and no different, the middle class being the middle class, from whitey.

Each morning I am at my desk by 8 A.M. Cover off the typewriter, I begin slaving away, typing charts. Not knowing how to tabulate, I just guess, reminding myself of the Incas who had no contouring instruments but trained their eyes to run a perfect line.

I am lodged between two women: Loretta Taylor, secretary to the administrator, with all the charm of one elevated to high authority; and a Mrs. Johnson, who apparently, like everyone else, myself included, reports to Miss Taylor. Each woman wears a new and different dress daily, while each day I wear the same costume: skirt and white blouse, worn flat shoes and no stockings. I have only one pair of stockings, and I save them for church. Perhaps there is pretentiousness in my unpretentiousness, but I have flown the world of pretense, of fancy clothes, and I want to get down to the essentials, to learn about "soul."

Above the clattering of the machine I hear Miss Taylor and Mrs. Johnson talking about a Miss So-and-so down the hall who doesn't wear stockings, she doesn't know any better, she says "stockings are so expensive," that she doesn't have the money to buy stockings, but she has a *professional* job, she *must* wear stockings, and "anyone with common sense knows this."

They keep talking, and all the while I keep hammering on the machine, listening, knowing: they mean *me*. There's no Miss So-and-so (the name always inaudible) down the hall. They are talking about me. Can she fire me for not wearing stockings? The horrible feeling of being on the "outside" of the "in" group, the group that knows what society dictates, what everybody does. My face feels as if I'd been standing in a blast furnace. *I have disgraced the office. I have pulled down the standards. Before I came, the office was a decent place.*

Finally, Mrs. Johnson leaves the room. "So," Miss Taylor says, "you *will* wear stockings tomorrow?"

You will comply! You won't go against society? This is the system, and within it we have found power. We make the wheels turn. We know how your legs should look. And if stockings are a must, might there be other rules: the length of a skirt? the styling of a haircut?

Cowed, beaten, feeling like a human being mistaken for a thing, I reply: "I get your message."

"It was no message," she replies. "I wouldn't say behind your back what I wouldn't say to your face." And I like her for that. She had said to my face what she had on her mind, while I don't have the guts to say to her face that I will not comply with her society-made rules.

When I close my typewriter and go out on the streets I realize the *apartheid* that exists even in this all-black community. The black women were holding up the standards, the values of the white System: conform, clothes make the man, be like others, act the role of what is "normal" and respectable. You don't have to think for yourself, but be like others; if everyone wears stockings, you wear stockings.

Like the militants around me I too want to scream "Hell, no!" to forces that would reduce us to cogs in a system that destroys individualism. Does the white man say the black militants are alienated? The black militants feel the one-sided emphasis on technique and material consumption has caused the white man to lose touch with himself, with life. And that it is he, whitey, and the Uncle Toms, the black man or woman who apes whitey, who is alienated, lost, lost from himself.

The next morning: I feel like a "dropout"; I do not want to face the good ladies who wear what they're supposed to wear. I'd rather be out on the streets, where so many Harlemites live their lives. I go to a telephone booth. I call Miss Taylor, tell her I won't be in. But I'm not so honest with her. If I were honest I'd say to hell with you and your stockings and your holding up whitey's standards. But instead I say I have another job.

Now again, I'm taking in the sights. Come along. Look at all the people, look at all the cars. You soon see that the automobile is as important as a status symbol to blacks as it is to whites, but the average Negro earns so much less than his white counterpart that he must remain in debt much longer in order to complete the purchase. You see that most cars in Harlem are for show only, since Harlem is not a big place and one can easily walk most places in the ghetto. And there are buses, taxis, and of course, subways.

Harlemites generally use their cars to drive a few blocks after work each day, from home to 125th Street, for instance, or to visit someone a short distance across town. I am always amazed when someone says, "I'll pick you up for dinner," and then discover our destination is only a few blocks away. Again it is the *style* of life that is important, even though the style seems more trouble than it's worth. Inevitably one has to circle the block, looking for a place to park, then frequently he runs the risk of parking in a no-parking zone or settles for double-parking, a custom prevalent all over Harlem.

With so much double-parking, the poor victims parked on the inside, by the curb, frequently find themselves hemmed in when they return to their cars. Enraged, they start blowing their horns for all they're worth. But how anyone can tell *for whom* the horn is being blown remains a mystery!

There's almost no place to put a car to get it off the streets. Harlem is a community of old turn-of-the-century brownstone apartment houses with no private garages. The streets are jammed day and night with old and new cars. And the stealing of automobiles has become a full-time job for countless Harlemites, many of whom are junkies who support their dope habits by any and all means possible.

Many Harlemites have installed sirens that alert police when a thief attempts to pry open a locked door. The result of this has been that the wailing of automobile sirens may be heard all during the night. Even so, the thieves are not easily deterred. One Harlemite bought a new convertible and installed the siren but the next morning his car was missing. "I later learned, when the car was found in a shambles," he told me, "that the thieves had sliced open the rear Plexiglas window and entered that way."

Harlem in some ways is like a cemetery: those who are "in" don't feel they can get out, and those who are "out" don't want to get in. The white people who own Harlem apartment buildings don't live in the ghetto; they live downtown. Slum dwellers, all with absentee landlords, come to feel that the masters of their destiny are faceless foreigners. Thus when they have a complaint, they find no one who will listen. And frustrations, repressed, have the capability of exploding one day.

The typical corner grocery is not much more than a hole in the wall, and all have meager, overpriced selections of food, most of it canned goods that won't perish. The meat, with yellow streaks running through the dull red, appears to be going, going, just about gone, all of it the type you or I would smell and then throw out.

As for the so-called fresh vegetables, I have never seen anything like them, except in garbage cans.

"How much is this head of lettuce?" I ask, in one store, holding up something the size of a tennis ball, which seems to have been on the counter for about a week and would never have gotten on the shelf of any store that sold to white customers. "Thirty-nine cents," the white man at the cash register replies. I hold up a half-dozen eggs. "Forty-five cents." In another store eggs sold for seventy-five cents a dozen, when in my Watergate Safeway store large Grade A eggs were selling for sixty-five cents. And a quart of ice cream, all over Harlem, sells for $1.50, while in Washington I can buy it for ninety cents.

The small stores seem never to have fresh fruit. Indeed, this was one of the rarest commodities in the ghetto. At a 125th Street open-air store, oranges are five for seventy-nine cents, while they sell twelve for sixty-nine cents at the Watergate Safeway in Washington. Lemons in Harlem are five for thirty-five cents, while Watergate Safeway sells them six for twenty-nine cents.

The ghetto's marked-up prices extend to *all* commodities:

cleansing tissues, toothpaste, the wetting solution for my contact lenses. Regardless of what I buy, I pay more in Harlem.
It is what Senate Commerce Committee Chairman Warren
G. Magnuson calls the "legalized thievery" flourishing among
the ghetto poor.

Why should the poor have to pay more for less? While the
current boom for white America keeps rolling along, the slice
of the pie for slum dwellers grows smaller. The ghetto poor
view America's uneven affluence with bitterness. The slum
poor can't buy the necessary staples such as milk, eggs, and
meat, yet they know that the Affluent Society has an excess
food production, with meats and vegetables in almost embarrassing surplus quantities.

When the urban Negro turns to riots he's making a protest
against this "legalized thievery" and all other conditions of
Negro life in the city, the garbage that isn't picked up, the
absentee landlords who refuse to fix the plumbing and eradicate
the rats. Most of all, he is expressing frustration at his in-
ability to attain economic emancipation. What he wants is
no great mystery: the freedom to *own* a part of America,
call it black pride, black identity, black capitalism, or what
you will.

How does one know a place? I open my pores, and say:
sights, sounds, atmosphere, this *here and now*, come to me and
live with me and be a part of me, as my arms and legs and
spirit are a part of me.

I begin to feel that I belong here, that I was born here,
that I will never leave Harlem. And, almost at once, the other
feeling: would I want to leave?

Yes, I love you Harlem because I have to love you. You
demand the choice; there's nothing else to do. You don't say:
give me 10 per cent of your affection, or 50, or even 100; you

make me go all the way, *200 per cent!* Yes, I have to love you or turn my eyes and look away. And unless I say I love you, then these streets, your people (and the city is the people, not all these buildings, all these businesses that whitey owns) would be ugly to me, and you are my people.

You have been condemned by those who don't know (who don't have any idea) how it is to live as you live. You are men wounded by being denied creative work; you are men given the right to hold a job but never the opportunity to own a part of the System. You are black women, not negligent mothers (who but black women could have held their families together under such circumstances for the past three hundred years?), but homemakers without homes, without a title, without even a mortgage. You have not failed so much as you have been failed.

. . . I came to Harlem alone, with my white mind and white spirit, and I will leave now a darker shade of *soul*. Harlem man, Harlem woman, I lived for a while among you, and I learned one thing: that under your circumstances I could not do half so well as you. It was hell to get into the ghetto, but now it seems that hell is outside—awaiting me, that place across the line, over on the other side of the black curtain— where I'm not supposed to go. Into whitey's world!

. . . Crossing over, coming downtown by bus, along Fifth Avenue, I see the pretty mothers with their pretty children in huge baby carriages, and the older youngsters with their nice blonde and carrot-colored *straight* hair, and I am acutely aware that within a few city blocks, two social orders live light-years apart.

For me the difference is not only that the slum is dirty and poor, while Park Avenue and Fifth Avenue are fancy, rich, aristocratic. There are the psychological barriers, which rise like impassable mountains between them.

The bus comes to Central Park and turns over to Fifth Avenue, my territory, my known quantity, my land, my people, my home.

I want to luxuriate in this Other World, and yet the insecurity of all that I have endured stays with me, a part of me, like the scabs on my legs, the dirt on my skin. I know that I have a key to the Good Clean White Apartment (relatives gave it to me years ago), and yet I check my pocketbook a dozen times, looking at the key. Ten minutes later I find myself again with the *need* to touch that key. It is the key to the other life—a precious link to escape and comfort.

I try to call my relatives. It is a Friday. They are in the country. I call a half-dozen times. I know they aren't there, but I feel myself untrustworthy; I feel that they would not like my slipping in. . . . Why do I feel that I would be slipping in? They have given me the key! If they answer, I won't go. I would not want them to see me as I am!

I need to get in the apartment, to take a bath, to feel that I am myself. I need to remove the mask, to make the change from black to white. (Mental, mental—except for the dirty rings that I will see on the tub.)

After the bath, I will inspect her closet—I will try on one of her nice dresses, I will feel the clean linens, I will remember that I myself have more than two changes of dress—that I have other shoes.

I am full of expectations and anxieties.

I am gawking. I become a tourist, wide-eyed, seeing it *all* as if I had been dead and resurrected, yet am unbelieving in the Miracle.

There is the Plaza, where I've stayed so many times. Yes, and later I lived there, on the fourteenth floor, overlooking the park. And there is Tiffany's, I've shopped there . . . and bought dresses and forty-five-dollar shoes at Bonwit's. My street . . . my world. . . .

But I'm not believing myself when I say these things. No, I am from the ghetto—when I say these things *to me* I might as well say to you that last Tuesday you drank a cup of tea with the Queen of England and then flew to the moon.

St. Thomas,
the Virgin Islands

Lying on the beach, I recall that when I first took the medication to make myself dark, a doctor told me, "You will be black for a year." But during my final days in Harlem I could see that I was losing some of my hard-earned dark pigment. I have come here from New York, to let the sun turn me dark again.

Mixing with the natives, who are black, I see them as proud, self-assured, beautiful people because no one has succeeded in convincing them that they are niggers. *The island is about 80 per cent black, 20 per cent white, which in one sense at least keeps the white man* in his place.

My last of ten days at Magens Bay, I hear from the central, thatched restaurant the voice of James Brown, "If I Ruled the World." And I think, Oh God, he is mine, a part of my world; I enter into his world. Yes, I know your streets. You are talking to me, brother. I know something about who you are, why you are as you are.

Tomorrow I go to another world, the South.

Part III

THE SOUTH

The South

In a New Orleans bus station, I ponder where in the South to begin. Since I don't know anyone, black or white, in the deep South, I figure one place is as good, or as bad, as another. Checking schedules first at Greyhound, then Trailways, I consider Montgomery and Birmingham, Alabama, and then choose Jackson, Mississippi, almost, but not quite on impulse. My recollections of Medgar Evers and Governor Ross Barnett and James Meredith make Mississippi at once more challenging and frightening than Alabama. I want to experience firsthand why so many believe it's the most backward state in the Union. As I pay the $5.90 for my bus ticket, forebodings like those that shadowed my approach to Harlem weigh heavily on me. And my own Southern-ness gives me no comfort.

Yet, because I am a creature, so to speak, of "the Confederacy," this trip represents an excursion into the past, a reliving of a part of my life, with glimpses into old secrets, long buried, yet still vivid and intimidating.

Now, sitting on the bus, a spook among spooks, as the whites sometimes call us niggers, I wonder: what will I do when I get to Jackson? Will I be able to find a colored guest house or a hotel room? The bus crosses Lake Pontchartrain over a bridge honoring the late Huey P. Long. My mind turns oddly to the figure of the Southern politician. Less a caricature of the string-tie Claghorns of the past, he still has a long way to go to become a model of enlightenment. All too often, he continues to thrive on prejudice and human weaknesses, exploited for personal gain.

With three or four exceptions, those aboard the bus are all black. When the bus rolls into a terminal only those who have reached their destination are permitted to disembark. In this way the blacks don't really integrate the terminals by using washrooms or restaurants. We are like prisoners, never being able to get off during a long journey to stretch our legs, buy a newspaper, or a cup of coffee. The basic needs of nature must be met in a small toilet at the back of the bus.

At Prentiss, a crippled Negro in his sixties gets aboard and limps to the seat beside me. He tells me his name, J. B. Lewis, and something about himself. He's been living in San Francisco for thirty years, has been back home visiting his father, ninety-seven. Of his visit he sighs:

"I'm as tired of these piny woods as a dead ox with his yoke. Could you ever live in such a place after you've seen other places?"

No, I assure him, I don't think so.

"I had these travelers' checks," and he draws some from his pocket, the same kind I'd cashed in Tangiers or Singapore. "Well, I went to the Prentiss bank, and the teller wouldn't cash them. He wanted to know *who* I was. I had to go several different times, and prove who my father was and who my grandfather was."

As we chat I ask J. B. if he knows a hotel or guest house in Jackson where I might spend the night.

"I'm staying with my sister and her husband, a Baptist preacher," and he invites me to go to their home with him. "But generally," he adds, smiling, "I try to stay away from preachers and other crooks." His phrase "preachers and other crooks" rings a bell and I remember that Longus Moore in Harlem had always talked as if the two were synonymous.

"This preacher, he's got *two* Baptist churches," J. B. tells me. "Drives a big Cadillac, yeah, they got a big house, lots of rooms." I hope it will be possible for me to stay in one of them, because I'm feeling alien and forlorn.

When we arrive in Jackson it's raining. We file off the bus, glad to stretch cramped muscles, happy for any shelter in the storm after five hours of sitting. But this "shelter" has less space than the bus. There's one room for waiting and for eating, at a quick-order stand with counter stools. Pay phones have no booths, no privacy. Everyone in the room with me is black. Glancing through a ticket-teller's window, I see another waiting room that is larger, more comfortable, with better facilities. It is for white people. Here in Jackson the signs "For Whites Only" and "For Colored" have been removed while in fact segregation remains.

A kindly Negro woman, seeing that J. B. is crippled, stands to give him her chair. At the pay phone, I check the directory for the name of Charles Evers, the person I want most to meet in Mississippi. The brother of the slain Medgar Evers, Charles returned to Mississippi from Chicago in 1963 and, in effect, said: Now here *I* stand. He aims to prove that while racists can shoot an individual they cannot kill the idea of free black men.

While I don't know Evers, I feel certain that if I can reach him he will help me.

The directory reveals no Charles Evers, so I dial information and a Southern white girl, after I've said the name three times, asks:

"What's the spelling of the last name?"

"E-V-E-R-S," I repeat.

"I have no listing for Charles Evers," she says in a way that leads me to believe she's never heard of the Negro civil-rights leader.

Back to the directory, I find an Evers, Mary. I don't know

his wife's name, but perhaps Evers, not wanting crackpot calls, has put the phone in his wife's name? I dial the number, and a woman answers.

"Is this the Charles Evers residence?" I ask.

"No, it is *not!*"

"Are you *related* to Charles Evers?"

There's a silence, a drawing in of breath and an explosive "We are *white* people!" followed by the bang of the receiver in my ear.

I return to J. B. We sit like two weary soldiers with our wounds. We await the Good Samaritan, the preacher brother-in-law, who will take us in.

"Perhaps I should call?" And J. B. agrees.

When the minister's wife is on the phone, I explain that J. B. and I have come in on the same bus, that he's waiting to be picked up; then I tell her that I've been unable to reach friends at the NAACP and that I need a room, just for tonight.

The Negro woman listens in the way that a Southern white usually listens to a Southern black: in silence, with mistrust and suspicion. Since there's no word from her end, I continue to plead my case. "By tomorrow I hope to find some of my family."

Icily she asks: "Just *who* is your family?"

Should I say the family of man? I specify: the Halsells, the Shankses.

"I don't know them," she says.

Hanging up, I return to J. B. "Your sister says the preacher's on his way."

Presently a large, dour-faced black appears outside the glass door of the overcrowded room, motions the crippled J. B. outside in the rain. He seems anxious to avoid the black rabble inside.

"There's the reverend," J. B. says and hobbles out. I watch them shake hands. J. B. gives the minister his baggage check.

After the minister walks off for J. B.'s bag, J. B. signals me to join him. Like two conspirators we go to the reverend's big white Cadillac. I help J. B. into the front seat, then climb into the back. "There's no reason why you can't stay with us," J. B. repeats. "It's a big house, plenty of rooms."

The minister returns, puts J. B.'s bag in the trunk, gets behind the wheel but makes no motion of starting the car. His silence speaks to me: get out of my car. "Reverend," J. B. says, "surely you can put her up, just for the night."

The preacher mumbles something about his wife being away from home and his own busy plans. I know from my telephone call that she is at home.

"Can't you take me to some widow's home? Any of your church members?" I ask resignedly.

He shakes his head.

I get out of his car, take my bag, and with a wan smile for J. B. walk into the rain. Trudging down a street, I neither know nor care in which direction I'm going. Strangely, I yearn for the rain to drench me. I want the physical discomfort. I hope it will overpower me, distract me from the painful misgivings assailing me.

A taxi pulls up behind me and stops as if ordered by some merciful dispatcher. I get in, and tell the black driver that I need to find a hotel. "How about the Summers?" he asks, and I nod agreement. Along the way, I think of the preacher, half in anger, half in pity.

What would it have cost him to take me in, just for one night? It would have cost him plenty. Reaching out to help a stranger, and all strangers in the South are suspect, he could be accused of harboring one of those rabble-rousers, one of those NAACP-ers, and, carrying the suspicion to its ultimate end, one of those Reds. It would have meant defying the unwritten but inflexible rules that no stranger comes among you unmarked. The preacher was frozen in the Southern mold, a captive of the mentality that rules the Old South: You're nobody, you don't even cash a traveler's check unless someone knows who your daddy is! J. B. and I, spiritually intact from our travels and knowledge of other worlds, have long since broken that mold, and life for us is freer, though one pays a price for being free.

The all-black Summers hotel provides me a room with the barest necessities: a bed, a low-voltage bare bulb dangling in stark ugliness from the center of the cracked ceiling, and the privacy of four blank walls. I walk from my room down a hallway to find the community bath and toilet. The door to the toilet does not lock, does not, in fact, even close, not by an inch or two, so that I feel exposed. Footsteps in the hall seem heavy, those of a man. They cause my heart to beat. Is *he* coming in here?

Apparently, I'm the only single, female guest. All around me are men, their voices coming through the thin walls. Listening to their talk, I wonder about their lives. Are they traveling salesmen? Are they young men from smaller country towns, in the capital for a few days on business of some kind? I feel as if I have been caught in a men's dormitory. The men are dressing for a night out on the town. "Man!" one calls exuberantly to another, "I'm gonna get me some real stuff tonight. None of that two-dollar shit!"

I lie exhausted, alternately dozing and waking to the babble of voices around me, and in the early morning, to roosters crowing from a nearby backyard.

Morning: I begin walking. All black people speak to me, accept me as their soul sister, while not a single white person nods a head, much less speaks. I keep walking, now in a white neighborhood. A house has a sign out front: "Room for Rent." I muster my courage, rap on the door, and am greeted by a white woman who studies me like an apparition.

"I'd like to see your room," I say. And I couldn't have shocked her more if I'd slapped her.

"I have no room!" She gazes at me incredulously.

"But you put out a sign."

"Why, you *black bitch!*" she shouts, and furiously slams the door.

Now, downtown Jackson, all brash, ugly commercial establishments, a memorial to the dollar. Nowhere can I find a park bench, water fountains, flowering shrubs, trees or signs that welcome, console, refresh and heal the weary spirit. I see a big church, with a sign out front: "Come, all ye who are weary . . ." But what would happen if I, a black woman, should enter that white church?

Walking the streets I realize the Southern whites talk loudly, raucously, while the blacks assume quiet roles of "invisible" men and women. To me, a black woman, Jackson seems barricaded, closed, off limits.

Waiting for a bus to take me back to the hotel, I stand among black women, as cold as I, with more problems than I. I know I must work as they work, immerse myself in their environment, scar myself with their griefs, if I am to end my sense of aloneness, of being on the Outside. I want to stand closer to them, to extract what I can from a physical togetherness.

Back at the hotel, finding no dining room, I go to a bar downstairs where the soulful voice of Otis Redding blares from a jukebox. I take a booth, order a beer and the house specialty, Southern fried chicken. A young Negro in slacks, turtleneck sweater, and Afro hair styling comes from an adjoining table of young men, all in their twenties, and asks if he can talk with me.

Can he talk with me! I'm in Jackson, sitting in that bar to meet him and others like him. Yet in the ambivalence that is female I struggle between being warm and friendly and being aloof, playing it cool. I can say, "Sure, sit down, I'm dying to know you." But I say nothing.

Taking my silence for consent he seats himself, tells me his name is Floyd, that he was born poor in the southern part of Mississippi, went to Chicago "and met this woman, she really dug me and I really dug her," that she was a prostitute, and that he pimped for her for a couple of years. "That was my bag," he tells me.

It rolls out of him, unprompted, as if someone else has wound him up and deposited him beside me to let him show himself off. Drumstick in hand, I keep my mouth stuffed with food and Floyd keeps talking, telling me of his teens when he played alto sax in an all-Negro band, and, "Man, all them white girls, they really dug me, they really dig Negro men; they'd come around and talk with me." But, he goes on, it's not true Negro men dig white girls. "They're the ones always running after us, me and most of my friends always running *from* them."

He says he could have "laid it out" in Chicago, living off the highly paid black prostitute, but that he'd come back to Jackson, where he now works in "public relations."

He tells of the prostitute and his two years of pimping by way of "introducing" himself to me, of *"telling it like it is,"* including the bad with the good.

I appreciate his attempt at honesty. To dare *say* what you dare *do* always requires some courage. Revelations, if one is sincere, not merely glib, can mean a giving of oneself; and gifts that reveal one's spirit are much more intimate than the undressing of the body. For this reason the naked soul and the naked spirit frighten us more than the undressed body.

Floyd speaks plainly because he is black. And in the world that white Americans have bequeathed to the black man there are no tidy, itemized alternatives, but only catch-as-catch-can, an improvised mode of behavior which requires the black to *create* ways of meeting adversities as he goes along. Talking as one black to another, Floyd assumes my understanding life as an almost insurmountable obstacle course. Naturally he'd grab any "bag" like a lifeline. He assures me he can understand my "bag," yet each time he prods for information, I steer the conversation back to him. At one point, he tries to pin me down, asking outright:

"Do you need to make any money tonight?"

He must mean something else. Is he proposing to find a paying customer for me? I reject the thought, but when I let my mind wander over what other possibilities I'd have for making money that night, I can think of none.

Goodness, I want to reply, are you still doing *that*?

"Can't it occur to you," I ask, betraying my irritation, "that a stranger can come into your midst without being a dope addict or a prostitute!"

"I didn't say that," he replies, gently. "You did."

He suggests we go to another place, "so we can talk more freely." Although I can't imagine *his* talking more freely, I agree to go. Outside he helps me into his late-model sports car, and we drive to another bar. He introduces me to an oversized young man called King who acts as though he owns the place. He escorts us to a black room, closes a door, and we're in total darkness. I hear fisticuffs and an awful ruckus back in the main bar. A woman screams and I hear a thud and imagine a body has fallen to the floor. A murder for sure. I visualize headlines about a police raid, with our picture on page one.

But no, all's quiet, and King assures me, "Just a lovers' quarrel." He switches on a pale, 25-watt bulb, and a half-dozen black men seem to materialize from nowhere and gather around a table, with me in the head chair. Their rather oblique talk gives me the uncomfortable feeling they're going to shoot craps, with me as the door prize.

But then I'm being naïve. King is the lord and master of the group, and any door prize naturally would go to him. He is whispering to one of his aides about having some "hot" fur coats to unload. Turning to me, he asks the most direct and blunt kind of questions. I brush him aside as I had done to Floyd earlier. "Why are you so silent about yourself?" he inquires. At one point, in a low voice, he asks, "Were you married, is that it? Running away from some guy?" I let my eyes water, as they almost automatically will on that subject. King reaches for my hand. "Shit! Grace," he comforts me. "Life's too short for that crap. Forget it! Forget him. You have to live *today!*"

I appreciate his gesture. But now I feel faint, unable to follow the words or general talk. I've come from other worlds, and the struggle to enter the Southern black milieu leaves me exhausted. I ask Floyd to drive me back to the Summers. En route, he tells me:

"Yes, I'd like to help you find a family and I've been thinking of my 'ontie.' She comes from an old *established* family, she's one of the leading citizens, but she'd ask you more questions than I've asked, and you'd have to have some answers, more answers with her than you have to have with me." He then suggests that I tell him the truth about myself, and that he and I can rehearse a story to give his "ontie."

Floyd parks outside the hotel, waiting for my story so we can convince his "ontie" that I come from a good family and am respectable even if alone in the world. But my mind's a blank. I'm utterly, emotionally, and physically drained. What am I doing in Jackson anyhow? Since there must be good, simple stories we could tell his "ontie" why hadn't I worked on them beforehand? I realize that Harlem had been easy compared with the South. In Harlem I was among blacks who have broken away from thinking like the white man. But here in Mississippi the black people are still shackled with what the white people teach each other: don't trust the stranger in your midst. And especially don't trust the black stranger. Floyd's "ontie" must believe that injunction as strongly as many Klansmen.

"I'll say goodnight," I tell Floyd. "If I don't find a place in a few days, I'll call you. Or look for you in the bar." He drives off, at high speed.

Inside the hotel a slight, bald-headed, almost toothless black man accosts me on the steps. "Do you need any stockings?" he asks furtively, adding that he can "slip" them to me.

"No, no," I assure him.

"Do you need *anything?*" he asks, and then informs me that he is going to "slip" me some money, that he wants me to have money in my pocket, that he doesn't want me worrying, going out looking for a job.

Who is he? How has he come into my life? Do I look so pitiful, so penniless, so destitute? Is *any* single woman in the black community considered so defenseless?

Then he states quite positively: "I know what you're up to." My mind reels trying to think of what he might be thinking I think I'm doing. But since at this point this is something I hardly know myself, I begin to feel I do not exist at all, except as a character moving around in *his* mind.

"You don't have *nothin'* in your room," he says. (Has he searched my room? But why?) "Tomorrow," he adds, "I'll 'slip' you a TV." His assurance that he can produce such bounty makes me guess he's the "manager," but he says no, he is the janitor.

Again he repeats, "I know who you are." I go on to my room, uncertain and worried about this intrusive man. I remember Thoreau's advice "I'd run a mile from a man coming to do me some good."

In my room, seconds later, I hear a rap on the door.

"Do you want a gun?" my self-appointed guardian asks.

"Do I want a *what?*"

"I can get you a gun. *For what you need to do.*"

Even Floyd, trying to identify my "bag," had asked if I were there to kill someone.

"Oh no, don't get me a gun," I tell him. I begin to feel enveloped. "I'll let you know *when I need it.*"

It isn't *things* I need, but someone, someone to whom I can talk, someone I can trust. Almost desperately I invite the meddlesome janitor, whose name I learn is Wash, the diminutive for Washington, inside my room, to take the one chair, while I sit on the bed. I ask him about King. "He drinks a lot," he tells me. "Might get to talking and also his wife can be real mean."

"It's not for romance," I say, "but just for a friend. And Floyd?" I ask.

"He's nice. But he'll *use* you, and break you and take all your money to boot."

Suddenly he starts to talk about his dead wife. "We was together sixteen years. You have a resemblance," he says, "except that she had much lighter skin than you."

Abruptly switching back to what he can do for me, he insists, "I just don't want you to have *any worries.*"

Yet I realize that he is accepting me as a person, with certain needs (and he's attempted to pinpoint them, stockings? money? a gun?) and with no pride to defend. Indeed, as a helpless female in a man's world, I decide that I am playing the role of a working black woman well enough if I evoke the desire of such a poor man to share his possessions with me.

"Why should you help me?" I ask. "I don't know *what I've done—*"

"Oh," he interrupts, "don't worry about what you've done. Your past is unimportant."

Before he leaves he wants me to stand close to his small, bony body, that is so emasculated in its crippled, aging condition. I comply with his wishes, realizing that people like the janitor and me and everyone, we "use" each other, and some are more honest about this than others. I don't know how I'll be able to "use" him, but I desperately want and need a friend. Meanwhile, I know I must get a job.

Early the next morning: I stand in the damp predawn wintery winds near a cluster of Negroes at the Capital Street bus stop. One man says, "Today week is Thanksgiving." At any time of celebration, the cry of loneliness becomes all the more acute. His words induce a self-indulgent inquiry: Where am I? What, why are we celebrating? An odd sense of detachment seizes me, the sense of being a foreigner in my own land. Thanksgiving, it means so much when one is a child. And then, grown up, everything changes.

Amid the shivering Negroes, a man, another woman, and I wait for the number four bus, and when it appears on the horizon we are like shipwrecked souls spotting a sail. We move to where we imagine the bus will stop and open its door, the door to warmth and the comfort of sitting down after forty minutes on our feet. We see that the bus is only half-filled with passengers, and, as always, the passengers are all black and the driver alone is white. We each clutch our coins, ready for that imminent moment of depositing them. The bus slows almost to a halt, but suddenly the driver guns his motor and the bus zooms past, leaving us incredulous. We shout and wave our arms in futile protest.

"Why, why would he do that?" I mutter aloud, and the other two would-be passengers, grim-lipped but resigned, show no surprise.

"Honey," says the woman, "*they* do what they want to do."

I want to be at the State Employment Agency by eight. Now I fear, having waited almost an hour for one bus, I almost certainly will be late. Another bus appears, and though it is not a number four and will mean a long walk for me,

I board it, deposit my coins and say to the white man at the wheel: "A bus passed us by! *Why* would he do that?" I might as well address the wind, so indifferent is the face before me.

I get off at the Old Capitol and walk several blocks to Yazoo Street, and to the neat, red-bricked State Employment Agency.

"I want to apply for a job," I say to a white woman back of the Information desk. She doesn't speak, doesn't "see" me, but hands over a card, and motions me to a high standing table where I write the particulars of my name, age, and type of job I want. Then, card in hand, I take my place among a group of black women, all seeking domestic jobs.

We are a dozen black women, some young, some old, others thin, a few fat. We are all talking, in low voices, on a common theme: the strange, inhuman ways of white folks.

"I works a full day for this woman," a maid relates, "and then she says, 'I don't have any money, you can come back another day and get it.' " The maid adds, "She knows I was coming. Why don't she have the money?"

Another tells of a white woman calling her to "leave your porch light on, I'm coming by to talk with you about a job." And, says the maid, "I leave the light burning until midnight for two nights in a row. She never come by, never call."

Still another says, "I was working from 7:30 in the morning to 5:30 at night for this family. It was always dark when I left home and dark when I got back. I hardly ever saw my husband. They paid me five dollars a day."

We are sitting, as children in a classroom. A fiftyish, pink-skinned lady with white hair has seated herself behind a desk up front, a desk with her name plate: Mrs. Hawkins. Her phone rings, and business begins. The phone has a white woman on the other end, who is calling to ask Mrs. Hawkins to get her a maid.

We have all deposited our cards on Mrs. Hawkins' desk,

and she picks one card and calls for a "Mary Sue Jefferson," who is a pretty, young mother with two of her six children, a boy, seven, and a girl, five. She tells the children to sit quietly and she walks up to Mrs. Hawkins' desk. When she returns to collect her children, I ask, "Did you get the job?" and she says yes. I wonder who looks after her young children while she works all day as a maid.

Then I hear my name. I am wearing a denim work dress, the old, worn shoes I had in Harlem. I shuffle forward (my feet, still swollen a size larger, don't fit in the shoes) and sit down in a chair in front of Mrs. Hawkins' desk.

"Grace," Mrs. Hawkins begins, "I have Mrs. Williams on the line. She wants someone for cleaning and ironing and will pay five dollars." I nod assent and Mrs. Hawkins adds, "She wants you right away, so she will pick you up."

I wait outside, at a "pickup" corner for black domestics, self-conscious, feeling I have a "For Sale" sign painted all over me. I've seen other pickup corners for men: one on State and another on Farish. The pickup corner is a throwback to the old slave market. Middle-aged and elderly poor Negroes stand each morning waiting for any kind of a job. A white man drives up, and usually choosing the youngest, most healthy man asks: "Wanna make three bucks?"

A Negro hustles to the truck or sedan. He has no idea what he'll have to do, but this being Mississippi he will labor eight to twelve hours before he ever sees the three dollars.

Now, at my pickup corner I see a woman driver slow to a stop. I open the front door: "Mrs. Williams?" and then, "Do you want me to sit up front?" She nods.

Mrs. Williams, in her late forties, wears blue stretch pants, a blouse and sweater. Her once blondish, now graying, hair is cut too short, too severe. She wears glasses, no makeup, and from the tension in her face, I assume she is a troubled woman.

We sit in silence, the kind a master imposes when he doesn't speak to his dog. Exceeding the speed limit, she races through the early traffic. I wonder if she does not wish her friends to see her with a black woman on the same seat beside her. Or maybe she simply wants to get the maid to her chores as soon as possible. When Mrs. Williams speaks it is only in questions. "Don't you have regular work?" And after I say no, and we say nothing for another five minutes she asks, "Have you looked for regular work?"

She stops at a Jitney Jungle supermarket and on her return thrusts a package of detergents and disinfectants on my lap. "Grace," she says, "I bought you some *tools of your trade.*"

The completion of one entire sentence that isn't a question so delights her that she goes off into guffaws of laughter. The humor of my scrubbing out her toilet escapes me, and I stare ahead unamused. Silence again rides with us. The gulf is broader than that between nationalities which have different languages. When she speaks, her tone and drawl are treaclelike, and her sugary intonation of my name makes me wince.

"Where do you live, Grace?" Her sweet, baby-doll dialect and her feigned defenselessness provide the armor of the Southern woman. Although aware that these weapons are hollow and harmless, I still am vulnerable to them. I am ambivalent. I have one emotion as a white person seeing her and quite another as a black woman seeing her.

My natural inclination is to smile and say "Where do you live, Jean?" And to ask other questions, such as, "Seen any good movies lately?" or, "Where have *you* worked before?" "Smart-ass" questions like that, I know, will get me fired before I start. Anyhow, I need all the energies I can muster for the chores ahead, so I respond only when she asks me something.

Once we enter her expensive home, she's in the role she knows best. Resorting to a harsher voice she barks commands like a field general. "Before you take off your coat," and she motions to a washtub near the back door, filled with clothes to be hung out.

I start to lift the tub, but she issues other orders: "First, take a damp cloth and clean off all the clotheslines." When I return, she directs: "I want you to sweep down all the walls, all the ceilings, then use this other broom to clean all the rugs. Use the dust mop on all the floors, this rag for the living room furniture, and this rag for the dining room furniture. And move the furniture to sweep behind the sofa and chairs. Polish all the mirrors, and then go over the glass on the pictures, and the glass of that china chest." On and on.

Long before I have one job completed there are new orders: "Now sweep off the front porch, the side porch, the back porch, and mop the back porch." The tone is unmistakably that of the mistress-slave relationship.

While I am "working like a nigger," Mrs. Williams talks on the phone, drinks coffee, smokes cigarettes, and complains to me about being tired. At first, I'd hoped I would be safe in my role as a Negro domestic. Then with some horror I learn that she is not capable of discerning in me anything other than what she assumes me to be, a lowly member in the caste system that perpetuates the easy way some Americans live.

I feel sorry for her. We are two women in a house all day long, and I sense that she desperately wants to talk to me, but it can never be as an equal. She looks on me as less than a wholly dignified and developed person. A huge pot of coffee is brewing, but she never suggests that I might stop, even for two minutes, and sip a cup. Actually I do not want the coffee but I ache to hear her make the gesture.

For my lunch, she puts a piece of bologna on two slices of white bread, places this on a paper plate, and says I should sit on a kitchen stool "and open yourself a Coke." She has everything designed so that my lips or hands will not con-

taminate any of her china or glassware, that nothing I touch
will in turn be touched by her lips or her hands. She goes to
the dining room to eat her lunch, making clear that she and
I both know my place. I have not minded the backbreaking
work (my father had drilled into me as a child that any honest
work is honorable), but I feel degraded by the paper plate, and
a new disgust with myself for placidly taking what the Negroes
call "all that white shit."

I have been seated for only ten minutes when she orders
me to bring in the clothes and start ironing.

After I iron a half-dozen sheets and pillowcases, a dozen
cotton dresses, a number of work pants and shirts, my eight
hours are up. She asks if I know where to catch the bus. No,
I say, should I turn left or right "when I go out the front
door"? The *front door* comes out inadvertently, because I am
only trying to get an idea of directions. She hands me five
dollars and ushers me to the *back door*, quite pointedly.

Two bus transfers and an hour later, I am back in "niggertown." Near the Summers hotel, young, bright-eyed Negro
children I've come to know wave, smile, or say "hi!"

I want to tell each one of them because I feel so degraded,
so morally and spiritually depressed, "Don't do what I did!
Don't ever sell yourself that cheap! Don't let it happen to
you."

And I want to add, "Even if you have to rob, sell your body
in another way, *whatever you do*, don't do what I did." The
assault upon an individual's dignity and self-respect has intolerable limits, and I believe at this moment that my limits
have been reached.

In the night: I am more than bone-weary. Muscles cry in
anguish, my feet throb. Will the enormous blisters bloom
again? I keep my feet elevated on the bed's headboard, hoping
the swelling will subside.

By 6 A.M. I am up, hurry to a bus for State Employment,

place my card on Mrs. Hawkins' desk, and sit down to wait. Nearly an hour passes. Walking to the front Information desk I ask a white woman, "Is there a ladies' room?"

She stares into space beyond my face. "We have one," and she gives a nervous laugh, "but it's for *us*."

A tall, attractive, brown-skinned girl, overhearing the conversation, says softly, "Come with me," and I follow her out of the State building, across a street, into an office building, down a labyrinth of corridors. I realize that as a black woman in Mississippi I can't even answer nature's call except in segregated discomfort.

"What kind of work you askin' for, *honey?*" the girl asks. When I say housework, she volunteers, "I've heard they're hiring at Jackson Steam on Alabama Street at $1.25 an hour."

"What about this minimum wage of $1.60?"

She laughs, "Well, you know how that goes."

"Yesterday," I tell her, "I worked all day and the woman gave me five dollars."

"Yeah," she replies, *"and I'd have gave it right back to her!"* Her anger growing, she adds, "I'd throw her five dollars *right in her face!*"

Back at State Employment, I wait until Mrs. Hawkins calls my name. She has a Mrs. Dunlap on the phone, who wants a maid "right away" for general housecleaning. "She'll pick you up," Mrs. Hawkins says.

On the corner, cars pass and several white drivers stop overly long, appraising me, as if I am For Sale to the white women or men of Mississippi. Seeing one young, pasty-faced boy staring at me from the comfort of his sedan and attempting a sickly smile, I am afraid I'll vomit if he doesn't drive out of my sight.

Waves of repulsion engulf me for the kind of life I am leading, not leading so much as merely sampling in the most cursory way. But if I feel cheap and degraded, very much like a prostitute (except that a prostitute could make far more per hour without any more humiliation than mine), then I wonder what must a woman feel whose entire life stretches out before her with no other prospect? Selling oneself all day long for five dollars! And to a woman keeping me in "my place"! A man might at least say a kind word. I know that if I had to continue being a maid for Mississippi whites, the work would not only destroy my body but break my spirit.

The Southern white lady no doubt might say: "Of course! A white person can't stand such labor, but the Negroes are made different, they are more like animals." I know that for myself alone I could not endure the work, but that as a mother I would make the sacrifice. Mothers who must somehow feed their babies don't get strength from their bodies alone, but from their hearts. I again think of the young mother, with the two children, seven and five, who had taken a job as a maid the day before. There must be tens of thousands like her, scrubbing floors to feed their children.

Mrs. Dunlap arrives. I see that she can be drawn in circles —round fat face, round fat body, and eyes covered with round dark glasses. Though she is built like a snowman, her features and demeanor have a certain hardness.

Like Mrs. Williams yesterday, Mrs. Dunlap does not talk except in questions. We speed to her home.

After we're inside, the phone rings and she gossips while I clean two commodes, two bathtubs, sweep the floors, mop the floors, make the beds, dust the furniture, and clean up after her teen-age son, whose penchant seems to be shelling pecans and drinking Cokes in bed. I clean the den, sweep and dust the room for the mother-in-law; clean the kitchen, run the sweeper in the living room, move the furniture, and sweep carport, front porch, sidewalks and the back porch. Finally she says, "I guess it's time for lunch."

She motions me to sit on a stool in the kitchen, and again,

like the day before, I am handed a *paper* plate. Dishes are everywhere, in several cabinets, and there is a dishwasher, so she is not giving me the paper plate as a labor-saving device for herself or for me, but rather as a device to keep me *in my place*. On the plate is a chicken-salad sandwich.

"I bought it at the drugstore," Mrs. Dunlap tells me. She takes a plate of cold roast beef and lettuce-tomato salad from the refrigerator and sits eating alone at her large dining table.

After lunch, when I'm again working, she sits in a large lounge chair to view an afternoon TV love-triangle serial. After this she finds me at my chores, and complains: "I couldn't sleep last night, I don't know why I haven't been able to sleep lately." Again and again she tells me she's tired. "I don't know why I'm so tired these days." But, I want to ask, tired from what? She's done none of the housework, none of the sweeping, scrubbing, dusting. She's only talked on the phone, watched TV, and given me orders.

Would she, I wonder, be less tired if she did her own housework?

I reflect that if Mrs. Dunlap loved her husband and child she could and would do the work I am doing. The soul song came to mind:

Oh you can't build a home with hammer and nails,
Bricks, mortar, and stone.
It takes love to make a house a home.

I scrub all the windows, noticing there's a brilliant, marvelous sun in that world beyond Mrs. Dunlap's dour countenance and her home that has the cheeriness of a funeral parlor. "You want the blinds drawn?" I ask, because they were drawn before I cleaned the windows.

"Yes," she replies. "And draw the curtains, also."

Suddenly I recall my childhood home, always bright with sunshine, bright with flowers, a tea kettle humming on a stove, and mother always singing, never tired, up at five or six, cooking, cleaning, washing, ironing, making all my clothes, taking care of her big family.

I look around this Dunlap house: no books, no magazines, no music, and yet the house must cost about thirty thousand dollars. It causes me to relive the richness of my own childhood. We were not poor! We were blessed with books and a piano (even if there were no rugs on the floor), with the good smells of mother's homemade bread and the freshness of washed, starched, and ironed organdy curtains. And the miracle of growing things, the sprouting sweet-potato vine encircling the kitchen window, the ten-cent package of seeds that turned to zinnias, marigolds, hollyhocks, phlox, verbenas, the bulbs that turned to hyacinths, tulips, daffodils.

In the afternoon I iron three washings—sheets, men's shirts, about a dozen dresses. Because I'm fairly fast, I finish the huge basket of clothes, at which point Mrs. Dunlap brings still more sheets, from last week's wash.

I grow faint and almost fall from exhaustion, but I recall that I had gone faithfully to the Health Club to build my body for such a crisis. I use a reserve of willpower, and like an intrepid mountain climber, I go on and on.

As I iron in the kitchen, she passes by several times, then sitting down with a cup of coffee, she talks in a manner that astonishes me. She spills over with revelations of a sexual nature about her husband, revelations that are so frank I find them embarrassing. He is a vastly inadequate man, she says. Then in still another confessional, he has a mistress he sees two nights a week. She is talking in a way I can't imagine her talking to any of her friends, even those she has known all her life. And she talks as if I am here and yet not here, in the way some people, when they are talking with one another, forget entirely that there's an elevator operator or a taxi driver or a waiter within earshot. "He" is there and not there. And so she talks as if I am here and not here, making me into some kind of Half-Person, or a kind of Non-Person. In this way she can say whatever she pleases with impunity, whereas with her best friend she no doubt would want to put her best self forward.

It is disconcerting to be treated, over-all, as a work animal, and then listen to intimate sexual revelations. I realize that regardless of what I might say, she is not capable of thinking, "Well, here's a kind of an intelligent *person*. What are her ideas?"

Since there is no give-and-take, my being only a listening post, I cannot imagine that her expositions of sexual frustrations and inadequacy serve as any value to her, provide any catharsis, since there is no response. The healing power of talk springs from the feeling that ideas are bouncing back and forth, that one wants and can accept the compassionate understanding of an equal.

If she recognizes that a Two-Thirds Person can tire, and long for courtesy, then she will have to recognize me as a human being. If I'm like her she will have to follow the old Golden Rule, and it can come down to her paying a person like me a decent wage, or cleaning her own commode. Inasmuch as her prejudices and tribal habits prevent her from going that route, she's stuck with trying to make the Myth the Truth.

The Myth means that as I move about, taking all her orders, the me of reality does not exist at all. Even if I quote Newton's laws or Einstein's theories she will "see" me only as she assumes me to be, a member of the caste system, a "Nigra" not her equal and one who is supposed to do slave labor while a few like her are not supposed to work. And this System is the way it is because God ordained it that way.

My feet throb violently from four hours of standing while ironing. I feel waves of pain. When you've stood, walked, bent, eight hours on your feet with only a ten-minute respite for a cold sandwich, particularly if you haven't ever in your life worked that hard, then you're a real clock watcher.

One, two, three, four, and the first half is over. Won't be long. Five, six, seven ("If I can only last another hour!") and I keep going, as fast as I can.

I finish all the ironing and am putting away the board at ten minutes before the end of the eighth hour, and she says "You're about through, aren't you?" "Yes," and then make the mistake of adding, because her voice is so sweet, "Is there anything else?"

"Yes, I want you to clean the oven." Her voice is still like syrup.

I almost break down. Luckily I control the tears. I get the steel wool and Bab-O (she doesn't have oven cleaner) and plunge my swollen, raw-red hands into the crusty debris.

When I am ready to leave, she says, "Would you like regular work out here? I've talked with my neighbors, and we can give you regular work, five days a week." I ask, "What would be the pay?" She says it would be six dollars a day. So, I can earn thirty dollars for a health-crippling, forty-hour, self-degrading week.

"I'll let you know," I tell her.

I want to get out of Jackson, to travel around Mississippi, to live with Negroes who will accept me as their loved one, their kin, their soul sister. Without an influential friend or contact in Jackson, I am stymied. I walk about searching my brain for a way out.

On Lynch Street, named for a well-known Negro, John R. Lynch, Speaker of the Mississippi House in 1872 and later three-term member in the United States Congress, I decide to make a move as obvious as it is pertinent. I head for the NAACP offices and I am met there by a Negro, sixtyish, erudite, sophisticated.

"Is Charles Evers here?" I ask.

"No, he's out of town." Then, "Can I help you?"

I realize I've gone as far as I can go alone in Mississippi. "Yes, please."

"I'm Alex Waites," he tells me. "Come in."

Because of my deepening sense of isolation and loneliness Alex Waites, kindly and solicitous, offers me a sudden comfort. He is quiet, restrained, a private man who spurns the limelight.

"I do need your help," I begin, having concluded that I can speak to him frankly and rely upon his discretion. He becomes one of a half-dozen private friends who share my secret. He is neither scandalized nor outraged by my confession that I am white passing for black, and he listens with sympathetic attention as I explain my desire to travel around the state, live with Negro families, and attempt to understand some of the problems in the small towns.

As we talk, I learn a little about Waites: that he is a native of New York, has lived all his life in the big city until, recognizing Mississippi as a challenge, he came here in 1965. "I've learned to love it here. Wait till you meet some of the Freedom Fighters," he says.

Waites promises he will talk with some of the NAACP people, including state president Aaron Henry in Clarksdale, and he urges me to "come back by in a couple of days."

I return. Waites says he has an idea. "You should meet the Hudsons in Carthage," he says. "They don't know what fear means."

The Hudsons, as Waites explains it, live in the same area where in 1964 three civil-rights workers were murdered. This preface is a warning of sorts, but Waites says that if I want to go there he'll call and ask Cleo and Winson Hudson if they'll take me in. "I'll tell them your story," he says. "If they agree, I'll drive you over there on Sunday."

While I wait in an outer office, he telephones the Hudsons. All is quickly arranged.

We leave Sunday about noon, driving through the piny woods of central Mississippi. "Most of the Hudsons and their relatives have much lighter skin than you," Alex tells me, adding that Cleo Hudson "will enjoy passing you off as his cousin." Also, he points out, "There's a Choctaw Indian reservation close by," and he chuckles over the prospect of white racists not being able to categorize me as Negro or Indian.

As we near Carthage, we read "KKK" signs painted into the concrete highway, indicating that the Klan is strong enough to boast even on public property. Alex, reading the signs, says of the Hudsons: "They've had to live with the Klan every day of their lives."

Now Alex and I leave the main highway, driving toward Harmony, an all-Negro community with fifty Negro families living on 35,000 acres of ground. Most of the land is covered with scrub and pine and not under cultivation. "They're supposed to meet us somewhere near a community store," Waites says, as we skid over red clay the consistency of molasses because of the constant rains. The woods seem surreptitiously astir with squirrels, partridges, dove, and deer.

We hear a honking, and a large woman, back of the wheel, motions us to stop. A tall, thin, caramel-colored man with a wide grin gets briskly out of the car and hurries toward Alex. They greet each other fervently, like brothers who have signed a blood pact.

Waites introduces Hudson to me and the tall man says with a cheerful lilt, "You're as welcome as the flowers."

We resume our journey and drive swiftly over the slippery roads to the Hudson frame house. As we get out of the cars, I meet Winson, a stout woman built on Russian peasant lines, and with a personality even more expansive than her girth. Waites already has told me she's Leake County's NAACP president, an active worker in the Head Start program for pre-school children, and head of the voter-registration project.

Immediately she leads the way to the kitchen, because it's warm there and there's food to eat. She has some ribs on the stove boiling. My eyes are mesmerized by a dead hog, from which the ribs have been sliced, lying in a tub on the kitchen floor. Although he's lost a few ribs he still seems to be alive and gazing at me as if judging me friend or foe.

"Just get a fork and hep yo'self," Winson invites us when the ribs are ready. They're as greasy as a can of lard for the likes of Waites and me, long bred on bland, cellophaned city food, but we fill our plates with the juicy, fatty morsels. The hog still looks back, accusingly.

As we eat, the Hudsons and Waites retell several of the most gripping accounts of Klan bombings and lynchings, and about the civil-rights workers, James Chaney, Andrew Goodman, and Michael Schwerner, who were murdered "just down that road a piece," after their release from the Philadelphia jail.

They talk about the Reverend George E. Lee, NAACP leader, killed by a shotgun blast from a car carrying several whites in Belzoni; about Lamar Smith, shot down on the lawn of the county courthouse in broad daylight after encouraging Negroes to vote by absentee ballot in Brookhaven; about Herbert Lee, a civil-rights worker shot by a white state legislator at Liberty; about Louis Allen, a civil-rights worker slain after testifying against a white man charged with killing a Negro at Liberty; Wharlest Jackson, NAACP leader, killed by the explosion of a bomb planted in his car at Natchez; and Vernon Dahmer, NAACP leader, burned to death in the fire-bombing of his home at Hattiesburg.

As they recount these acts of terror, all in Mississippi, I listen like any interested yet *detached* observer. Then I see that Alex is rising and walking to the door, and suddenly I feel like the child of five when Mother had taken me to Grandma's and was leaving me there, away from her, *out there*, with all that I did not know. "Have some more ribs, *cousin*," Hudson says, probably divining my thoughts, and he smiles at me with his twinkling eyes.

After Waites leaves, the three of us continue sitting around a small kitchen table, in earnest, get-acquainted conversation. Actually, the Hudsons do most of the talking.

Winson tells me about her sister, Dovie Hudson, "we married cousins," a widow with eleven children, who filed the first school desegregation suit in the area.

"Dovie's home was bombed twice," Winson says. In November, 1967, "The Klan was backing into our house to throw off the bomb. Our only daughter was living with us while her husband was in Vietnam. She was sick that night, was expecting a baby. Cleo and I ran out in the yard, to start shooting. Our German shepherd dog was after the Klan, barking and forcing them to move on.

"I ran to the phone to call Dovie to be ready. When she lifted the receiver I heard the bomb go off—at her house! I heard her little girl screaming, 'Oh mama! Oh mama!'

"I ran out of the house, intending to run the two miles to Dovie's house. Cleo was firing, emptying every bullet in his shotgun.

"Our daughter thought it was the Klan, firing on us. She ran after me, grabbed me around the neck, trying to get me back in the house. I pulled loose from her to go on to Dovie, and she fell on the concrete porch. Then I heard her moaning, 'Mama, I'm hurt.'

"Cleo and I rushed her to Hinds General Hospital. The baby had to come. The baby was premature, had to stay in the hospital a long time.

"That same night," Winson went on, "my daughter's husband was guarding the Cambodian border and was wounded. He was hit three times, in his leg, in his knee, and in his chest.

The bullet in his chest is near his heart and will remain there for as long as he lives.

"I'll let anyone decide within himself how he feels about his country that he was defending, how he feels about the country his son will grow up in."

The next evening, after we'd eaten more of the hog, Carlee Johnson, a farmer, his attractive wife, Marie, and three of their ten children come by for a visit. Cleo introduces me as "one of my cousins." We chat for a while and then Cleo, lowering his voice and pledging the children to keep a secret, reveals to the Johnsons that I'm not really his cousin, and tells them I'm passing as a Negro to learn how whites treat the blacks in Mississippi. "You'll sure learn a plenty," Marie Johnson volunteers.

We all begin talking quietly, as if we are in the catacombs, willing to face the lions or any death before giving up our faith. This could be some clandestine cell meeting, rather than "free" Americans gathered in a living room. Like a sheaf of grain, weak as one stalk but resilient and strong when bound together with others, we experience a new kind of strength.

They all want to help, but how? "If the Klan finds out where you're staying, they'll kill us and you," Winson cautions. "If there's anything them peckerwoods hate worse than a *nigger* who talks back to them it's a white woman living with the *niggers*."

"Yes," Cleo agrees. "If your secret gets out in Carthage, you not only will never get a job, washing dishes or scrubbing jobs or nothin', you'll be lucky getting out of here alive."

The next morning the Hudsons and I eat breakfast, with the hog still with us. We leave early for the drive into Carthage, they in front and me in the back. Long before we enter the city limits, they instruct me to crouch in a hidden position on the back floor so that no Klansman can see me and become suspicious.

They point out that while white racists do not see Negroes as people, as human beings, they nevertheless are acutely tuned in on moods, changes, new faces in town. The stranger likely will be working for the NAACP, voter registration, Head Start, and this means, to the racists, that the stranger is a rabble-rouser, a Red, or a traitor.

The Hudsons park behind a service station. I'm still lying on the back floor. They tell me they see Johnson parking, some distance away. Marie Johnson gets out, takes her smallest child, about five, and walks slowly to a designated place. Meanwhile, on a cue from the Hudsons, I escape from my hiding place and begin walking. I'm to walk slowly, make a casual "accidental" encounter with Marie and then begin with her the stroll toward the courthouse.

We feel that the eyes of all the white men are upon us, judging us, weighing us, measuring, appraising. It is worse than being judged and *priced*, because in the eyes of these men we are theirs by birthright. By being born white they automatically have us as their property.

If a white man wants to cross in front of us, and several do, we step back, and if a white motorist wants the road, we yield briskly and without question, for a black pedestrian dare not assert his rights.

We pass rows of stores whose owners, all white, refuse to hire black men or women, no matter how menial the task. The only way a black person goes in those stores is with money in his pockets, and then he's "free" to spend his money, and get out, and back *in his place*.

Caught in this climate of hate, I am totally terror-stricken, and I search my mind to know why I am fearful of my own people. Yet they no longer seem my people, but rather the "enemy" arrayed in large numbers against me in some hostile territory.

I remember that I've walked in Communist Yugoslavia when almost no Americans went there, and in Communist East Berlin, knowing that back of some drawn curtains eyes peered at me. I've been among those "Reds" in Russia, living alone in a hotel, wondering if my phone was bugged, if my mail was read, if strange, armed men followed my every step. And yet none of those experiences prepared me for this march to the Carthage courthouse.

My wild heartbeat is a secondhand kind of terror. I know that I cannot possibly experience what *they*, the black people, experience, walking through that cheap façade of manhood, dedicated to preserving the whites' hollow "superiority." The atmosphere seems charged, an atmosphere made ready for terror and violence, sanctioned by the community, against any uppity nigger. But how much deeper the hate would be if they but knew that I was one of them, a Southern white woman here to expose and illuminate their prejudices. There is no pride like that of a hateful white Southerner, and he cannot abide his white woman in the company of blacks. It is purity and chasteness defiled.

Marie Johnson and I walk slowly, deliberately, as in the cowboy movies; it is a kind of *High Noon* for me, and I am completely defenseless. Mrs. Johnson, holding on to the staged decoy, the child, barely able to toddle, moves almost as if in slow motion, and I am at their side. How easily I have sunk into a cowed, subservient, fearful creature simply because it is expected of me, a black woman.

We pass a large tinsel Christmas tree, as tall as the two-story courthouse, and go into the building, climbing to the second-floor State Employment office, where we take seats beside two Negro women, waiting to be interviewed. I notice a large poster, sent from Washington with firm instructions to display, stating that "No Discrimination Is Practiced Here." Below that phrase, composed in good faith by someone far removed from Mississippi, are faces of Americans of diverse cultural backgrounds, black, white, and Oriental, smiling in happy togetherness. Here it is a mockery, a grim joke.

A pasty-faced woman of perhaps twenty-five, her fingernails bitten to the quick and speaking nervously in the cloying accent of the Mississippi white woman, calls the Negro women one by one to her desk for interviews. Instead of job qualifications we are asked: Have you ever been active in voter registration? You're not having anything to do with that Head Start program, are you? Have you had anything to do with any of those NAACP agitators?

Marie Johnson has coached me: "You *have* to tell them *no*. I goes ahead and tells 'em no, because it's none of their damn business anyway. They play me for a fool, I plays them for a fool."

The white woman calls me forward, without ever looking at me. I know it is beyond her wildest imagination to think of me as anything but a person beneath her.

Preliminaries aside, she asks, "Would you like factory work?" Before I can assure her I'll take it, she adds, "The main factory is closing down for the holidays; there's not anything available now," and then she goes into a nervous little chuckle.

"It'll be *at least* two weeks before I can possibly turn up anything," she says, giving the answer the Hudsons had predicted: no job of any kind until your political affiliations are investigated by the Klan and other white racists.

Pretending to be destitute, I ask about getting welfare assistance and am directed to the floor below, where a woman in spike heels places me out in the general hallway with the spittoons and passersby. I sit for half an hour, time enough to wonder about the lives around me, the clerks returning from their coffee break, idly gossiping. No white person looks at me, sees me. I'm behind a glass, as it were, that enables me to see out while they can't see in. After some time, the woman in spike heels returns, writes down my name and other details. I'm now turned in on myself, dour, depressed, and I lapse frequently into silence, give glumly muttered answers. Finally, she asks in the form of a declaration, "You must be Choctaw, aren't you?" And without waiting for an answer she writes "Indian" on her paper.

The woman seems now to evidence a new degree of interest in my welfare, but she stresses that no one can get any Mississippi money unless he or she is ancient, has about a dozen dependent children, is blind, or on death's bed.

"And you *are* able to work?"

"Yes," I say for the ninth time. "I'll take anything."

I continue sitting while she teeters over me in her spike heels, and she finally grows tired of the catechism. "Well," she says, "we could give you *a few commodities*," throwing out the suggestion as if tossing a bone to a contentious dog.

"Commodities, that's a sack of flour or a sack of cornmeal, what we call 'hush material,' " Cleo has already explained to me, adding that if the Negro really starts complaining about his dire circumstances the welfare authorities will say, "Go over and get some commodities."

But the commodities are promised to me only if I try harder to find work, and failing, report back to Welfare in a week or two.

Leaving Welfare, I go downstairs where I find Mrs. Johnson and her child sitting on a concrete slab by the steps, eating grapes. Other Negroes are there and I join them. We stroll over to a store where Mrs. Johnson buys the baby a pair of shoes, and then we join Carlee, who drives us to the spot where the Hudsons are waiting for us.

"We just have to get home to that hog," Winson says. We three return and settle in the kitchen, with Cleo cutting up a tubful of pork for sausage and salting down the rest. Winson is on the kitchen phone, and I heat buckets of water and wash the dirty dishes.

As we move about our chores, I remember that nothing is more conducive to talk than an old-fashioned kitchen, with confessionals springing from the soapsuds and the preparation of food for the winter months.

Cleo talks about the civil-rights workers:

"These kids, it was the first time that whites came to our homes, lived with us, ate with us. Sometimes we had so many here at night you'd have to be careful where you stepped, they'd be sleeping on pallets on the floor, anywhere, they didn't worry about their comfort.

"Winson and me, we'd always thought we were militant, but these kids went around daring the officials. What really bugged the white people worse than anything, worse than maybe if they'd gone out and started shootin' and killin' people, was that these kids, black and white, walked around together, and seemed to be having fun, enjoying theirselves. And the whites, they couldn't hardly stand this. And when two white boys were walking down the street with a Negro girl, she was from New York, the white men citizens here, several of them, jumped on them, and took them, locked them up at the jail-house, and then nearly tore all of them to pieces."

Cleo keeps cutting up the hog and at one point he makes an analogy: "See what this salt does to this hog, it saves it, and this is what you do for me and I do for you."

Suddenly, in his random musings, he blurts out, "Grace, could you marry a Negro man?" and he goes on to say that he had asked this question of a young girl, a civil-rights worker from New Jersey, who told him, "Well, we go together, I mean black boys with white girls and black girls with white boys, but no, I couldn't marry a Negro because it'd mean too many problems."

I keep Cleo waiting for my answer and then I reply, Sure,

but that I hope I will never do it as a rebel's cause or out of any idea of love for an entire race, which to my mind isn't possible. Just as so many Southern white girls are repelled by black men, they also can be quite attracted to them, and vice versa, and I have heard of marriages in which the black man and Southern white thrash out their inner conflicts with wild arguments, the girl passionately loving the horsewhipping she takes to expiate a Southerner's past sins.

All that is buried and secret and awesome about sex carries over today as the crux of so much of our national dilemma. The white man denied the black man his dignity a long time ago, and the white man started sleeping with the black man's woman, and the white man told the white woman the black man was a sexual giant, and he told the black man that he'd kill him if he even *looked* at a white woman. What results today is that all those taboos have come home in a simple truism that opposites attract, or, you sometimes want what you're not supposed to have.

But if you are mature enough to know yourself, live your life for yourself, and not society, then you are freed from being attracted or repelled because of, or in spite of, a person's color. In a word, you're home, *free*.

It's only because of the sins committed by white men in America more than three hundred years ago (and steadily ever since) that the question looms with any significance. Cleo didn't think to ask, could you marry a Korean? a Peruvian? an Italian? a Baptist? a Jew? a Moslem? All such questions, except the black-white theme, today seem rather provincial. I am disappointed in that young girl from New Jersey who'd traveled all the way to Mississippi and then confessed she wouldn't want any *personal* problems by marrying a Negro. To rule out love because it'd create problems, that's ruling out a lot of life.

After getting the hog put to rest, Cleo, arming himself with the shotgun, asks me to go along for an instructive drive. "You see how poor we are. Now I want you to see some really poor folks," he says. Heading for the home of Mrs. Clement Johnson, a widow with fourteen children and no income other than ninety dollars a month from welfare, Winson warned, "Be careful not to step in one of the many holes and break a leg. Walking in her house you can always look through holes to the ground beneath and through other holes to the sky above." The few scraps of furniture in the house and the clothing on the children are donations that Winson has somehow managed to find for the woman.

We later visit an Indian woman, Ethel, thirty-seven, whose oldest daughter, fifteen, comes in while we are there. She is butterball fat, like her mother, as round as she is tall. She has been attending the Carthage white school, but some white parents complained that the Indian girl is pregnant, and she has been expelled. Ethel insists, however, that "I took her to the doctor and she's not pregnant."

Ethel obviously does not practice racial discrimination. While the fifteen-year-old girl is by an Indian father, Ethel has a sleeping baby on the bed by a white father and in her arms holds another baby, six months old, sired by a Negro father. Ethel said to Winson, "This here'n is half mine and half yourn."

Winson, her motherly love growing expansive, urges, "Ethel, let me have this one!" Ethel turns to Choctaw language, causing Cleo and Winson to laugh at her rebuttal. Ethel has told the Hudsons that a white welfare worker, incensed at her indiscriminate love-making, has threatened to take the children away from her, but Ethel jumped on the woman, beat her with her fists, until she left screaming. And she hasn't returned since.

We go back home, and eat more of the hog. After four days, I decide to give up on finding a job here.

I return over the same route that Alex Waites has driven

me, now by bus, to Jackson. where I go "home" to the Summers hotel and call Waites. He says that Charles Evers is now in Jackson, "and I told him your story." I walk over to the NAACP offices and Evers, standing, embraces me with a bear hug, affectionately calling me "You, you Indian!" He's heard that the Carthage Welfare office has mistaken me for a Choctaw.

"Have you had lunch?" he asks. It's 3 P.M., and I've eaten, but I agree to accompany him. He takes a .38 pistol from a desk drawer and puts it into a holster he wears under his jacket. In his car he places the pistol on the seat alongside him. When we leave the parked car to enter the restaurant, he again puts the pistol in his holster. "I'm never without a gun," he says, adding: "I hope it doesn't bother you."

"No," I say. "I feel better knowing that you have it." I am mindful of the small irony of feeling better that a black man is armed and will protect me against the whites. But only by being a black among blacks can I sense his need of being armed, and my own sense of security that he is.

There's a midafternoon lull in the colored-owned restaurant when we enter. We sit in a booth and he orders several "soul food" specialties. Even as he eats he talks, and I hang on every word, fascinated, saddened, sometimes sickened.

The impact that young civil-rights workers had on Mississippi in 1964 was revolutionary and shattering to the "closed society" of that benighted state. Evers' matter-of-fact manner conceals his own deep emotional response to it.

"In small towns like Carthage and even Jackson it was startling for white citizens to see black and white young people living their lives without any concern for the color of their friends," he says. "To tell the truth, I too was startled, because it was the first time it had happened in Mississippi. I would think: I wish them well, I hope they don't get into any serious trouble, I hope they escape with their lives.

"A thousand kids came to Mississippi and they walked up and down the streets, blacks and whites, holding one another's hands. Most of the white people couldn't swallow this integration, but they had to keep on taking it. In other words, we developed what Aaron Henry calls the 'puke theory.' We gave the white man so much integration that he just heaved it up, kept swallowing and heaving, until he got so he could kinda stand it, and his stomach doesn't bother him so much now when he sees blacks and whites together."

Now Evers turns to the white man's centuries-old practice of taking black women for his carnal desires. "The black man has seen this happen for more than three hundred years," he says. "The practice has 'emasculated' the Southern black man," he asserts. "The black man's got to start wearing *pants*, he's got to put some starch in them. Start being *a man*."

He recalls his growing-up days with his younger brother, Medgar, who was killed in 1963 by a white racist.

"We were always so close, and we always vowed that if anything happened to one, the other would take over," he says.

At first they started out hating the white man, he recollects. "We used to plan, lay awake nights, planning how we'd go out and on our own kill two white men for every black man that was killed. We were just going to take this upon ourselves. And we were going to store rifles, and we had a plan where one would drive the other to a scene and then leave, by car, and the other, who did the killing, would come back by bus so no one could trace him.

"Our mother was a wonderful Christian woman, one of the ones who used her religion for good, not evil. And she somehow knew what we were planning, knew without knowing, in the way a mother does. And she kept praying for us. 'Son, I'm praying for you,' she'd say to Medgar and me, and that's all, or 'Son, I want you to learn to love, not to hate,' and this somehow got through to us, her message that you can't win anything by hating, that one killing only leads to another and another.

"Medgar stayed here and worked in civil rights, and I went to Chicago, and was in business up there, but when he got shot, I came back immediately and knew I had to stay. I'm trying to carry on what he started. I want my work to be a monument to Medgar. He was really loved by the people of Mississippi, and they knew him, all of the ones who are fighting for freedom, knew him like I did: like a brother.

"There's two things we blacks have to get, and one's the vote, that's real black power; and the other is green power, economic control of some of the land, of some of the businesses.

"The vote is going to change everything in this state. And this is a good state. I believe the black people will stop leaving Mississippi. It's our homeland and we love it as much as the whites. We can learn to live here in peace.

"In fact, I think the Southerners, the Mississippians, are further along the road of solving racial problems than the white and black people of the big cities. Here we come in contact with each other every day, we're used to living close to each other, we know each other, we know each other by name and by our little failings and our little victories, and when this white man of Mississippi comes around, he's really your friend. Sure, we're going to live together in peace in Mississippi, and it's gonna be sooner than most people think."

After he finishes eating, we drive back to the NAACP offices. He goes into a conference meeting, and I talk with Waites, who is arranging by telephone for me to stay with active NAACP workers in outlying regions of the state, such as Indianola and Clarksdale in the Delta.

"I've told Carver Randle, the Sunflower County NAACP

president in Indianola, your story, and also Aaron Henry, in Clarksdale," Waites tells me. "They'll be expecting you, and will help protect you, as best they can, from the white racists." It is strange, I think, that I must ask the black people to help me defend myself against "my" white Southern brethren.

The next morning I board a bus for the Delta, an area of rich land and poor people, in the northwest corner of Mississippi. The towns all seem self-contained, barricaded against strangers, fretful, and lonely. Yet across the main streets of each of these ugly little citadels of white supremacy hangs red, green, and silver tinsel, like proud necklaces, and loudspeakers blast to a misty sky: "Peace on Earth. Goodwill toward men." The message mocks reality, for Mississippi's equally divided people, about 50 per cent white and 50 per cent black, know little peace. The bunting and the blare conceal a hateful world in an unraveled condition. Within the black group, a hard-core group of dedicated men and women live and die for freedom, newly minted and defined for them by Alex Waites and Charles Evers in Jackson, the Hudsons in Carthage, and scores cut from the same brave mold.

When the bus stops at Canton, an elderly but spry woman sits down beside me. She's been visiting a daughter in Canton, and now is going back home to Greenwood.

As the ancient Trailways bus rolls along at an arthritic pace, wheezing and sputtering at each change of gears, the woman, who introduces herself as Mrs. Tinie Parker, talks of her children, grandchildren, and of her dead husband. She giggles when she tells me a widower, knowing that she has a little property, has proposed that they get married, "but I'm too old for all that nonsense."

At Winona, a remote dusty stop along our route, we all stumble off to change buses. Again, it's the now-familiar routine of entering a small, stifling waiting room with no comforts provided the travelers. This one has a half-dozen chairs discarded from a classroom. The chairs, designed for six- to ten-year-old pupils with writing table on the right side, are small and ridiculous-looking in the bus station. Yet the white operators must consider them suitable for bus passengers, most of whom are black and presumably adaptable to children's desk chairs or any other corporate indignity.

Mrs. Parker or any of the other travelers would be miserable and look grotesque squeezed into one of those chairs. She rests her packages on the writing side of one of the chairs, and we look around. There's not even a food or drink counter where one can climb upon a stool and order coffee or a Coke. No, we are in Mississippi, where a white man operating such a café will be required under federal law to serve *all*, blacks and whites, side by side, on counter stools elevated the same distance from the floor. Even the rest rooms are open for only fifteen minutes after any given bus arrival, which means that one answers nature's call at the convenience of the white citizens of Winona.

Since Mrs. Parker and I have about an hour's wait we stroll outside to a nearby milk bar, and are near the take-out window when an irate white woman, for reasons unknown to Mrs. Parker and me, attempts to dislodge us from the counter window.

"*You* are not supposed to be at this place, place for you is 'round yonder!" She motions to a back window where several Negroes are being served, but neither Mrs. Parker nor I have seen this back window for "niggers."

Mrs. Parker and I ignore the white woman and give our orders for milkshakes and doughnuts. "But what's the difference, really?" I ask the white woman. "We're all just waiting. . . ."

"I don't want to talk to *your kind!*" she screams, and when the blonde girl back of the take-out counter ignores her and proceeds to serve black people, she turns on her heels and marches off, muttering. She leaves me wondering how many millions of "free" white Americans there must be like her, whose hatred for blacks shields their insecurities.

The next bus arrives, and Mrs. Parker and I board it with relief and continue on toward Greenwood. "Greenwood," I say. "Isn't that the home town of Beckwith, Byron de la Beckwith?"

"Yes," she replies, "and I've seen him many times." In the small community of Greenwood, he is a familiar figure to everyone.

"He's a fertilizer salesman," she tells me. "A member of the White Citizens Council. The gun that killed Medgar Evers was traced to him. He was charged with the murder of Evers, but he's had two mistrials. And there's never been a case in Mississippi where a man tried twice has been tried three times. So I guess there's no possibility of Beckwith's being tried again. He's walking around on the streets, now, a free man.

"He's in his mid-forties, a short man. Everybody knows he collects guns. He carries a shotgun. Likes to fire it. Says to groups of whites, out loud for all to hear, 'We know how to treat niggers in this state!'"

"And," I ask, "didn't he even run for Lieutenant Governor?"

"Yes," Mrs. Parker replies, bitterly. "And won a lot of votes, too."

At Greenwood, Mrs. Parker gets off the bus and is met by one of her sons.

I am all the more alone and apprehensive as I travel on to Ruleville. I'm following a schedule made by Alex Waites that will let me see as much of the state as possible, and arrive at the Indianola Greyhound bus station at an hour convenient for Carver Randle to meet me.

In Indianola the bus pulls off the highway ten minutes early, stopping in front of a concrete-block structure of crackerbox design. It protrudes from the landscape in raw, stark nudeness, there being no trees or shrubs or adjoining scenery of any kind.

"Dixie Welding Supply," a sign announces above the building, and underneath in smaller letters, "Greyhound Bus Station."

I stand in the cold wind, studying every face and seeing the Negroes who have gotten off the bus move away with families or friends who have met them; then departing passengers board the Jackson bus, and it takes off. I can see no one who might be Carver Randle of the NAACP, who has agreed to meet me, according to Alex Waites. I know the bus is early and there's nothing to do but wait and hope for the best, that is, that Randle will appear.

Still I am freezing! I've seen two Greyhound bus drivers marching in and out of the Dixie Welding Supply, so I step inside the entrance. I am standing just inside the door, looking through a plate glass, alert for Randle, when I hear a woman almost spit in my direction:

"What's she doing in here! *Git her out of here!*"

As a white woman, I've never been spoken to in that tone of voice, and it momentarily stuns me. Shock might be a better word for it. I stand glued in my tracks, undoubtedly looking cowed and stupid.

"You can't stand in here!" a white man, obviously the owner or manager of the store, shouts at me. "*Now git out!* There's a place for your kind, around the corner."

Cold, lonely (even good bus stations are lonely), and confused, since I've seen the two Greyhound bus drivers tramping freely in and out of the office where I stood, I nevertheless have been told to "git" in such a forceful way that like a beaten cur I "git."

In a "waiting room" about the size of a broom closet, two black mothers with their children are sitting on a bench (no chairs). There is scarcely any space to stand, but I crowd in anyhow, elbowing into a cluster of blacks and grateful for the warmth and shelter. I glance around for a rest room, and my eyes don't have far to wander. There is a rest room, but the door bears an extra-large, neatly printed sign announcing "Out of Order," which the Mississippi blacks take to mean: "For Whites Only."

Adjoining this door is another door, with a cut-out window that opens and closes and provides enough space for a white man on the inside to reach his hand through and take dollars from the Negroes on the other side in exchange for bus tickets. It is all ingeniously planned, with the whites safely walled away on the other side of the trapdoor never needing to see or come in contact with the Negro passengers, who have no café, no rest room. So the whites never have to touch anything that *them niggers* touch.

I rap on the trap window and the face of the white man who has ordered me to "git out" appears. When I ask, "Where is the telephone?" he replies vehemently, "There's not one! Can't keep one in that waiting room. You damn niggers tore it off the wall." Like an accused person who begins to waver in his belief of innocence, I look to the wall to see if a phone has been there, but I can't see that it ever has.

I go outside again and look for Carver Randle. A bus driver, tall, gaunt, a large hawk nose on his thin, sickly, white face, strolls into the supply office. I am tired of that cold wind biting into me and ache at thought of the heat inside. I venture to the main "white" door again, but discover to my shivering dismay I have been locked out!

Back to the colored waiting room, and to the door with the trap window. I open this door and walk into the office, nothing more than a cheap, country store, with no furnishings other than the barest necessities.

"May I use that phone?" I ask a woman seated behind a desk. She's the same white woman who earlier has shouted, "*Git* her out of here!" Now my effrontery in again showing my black face causes her almost to choke in anger. She shouts:

"We *told* you you're not supposed to be in here!"

"Well, I have to use the phone," I say, and at this point I can't think black or white, but only that I am very tired. "I have to ask if someone is going to pick me up."

She eyes me with the abhorrence of a criminal, of one who'd rape a nine-year-old child. I've never seen a face twisted by such hatred. Finally, she asks, icily:

"What number do you want to call?"

She obviously assumes that I am a black maid waiting for the master or the master's wife to pick me up at the station. I give her Carver Randle's home telephone number and she dials it, marking each digit with tremendous force.

Then she will not hand me the phone, but asks, "Who's waiting to be picked up? What's your name, *girl?*"

But why won't she hand me the phone? Will my black hand on the instrument leave so much blackness that it will rub off on her? Will I never be allowed to touch what she touches? Does my very presence contaminate the air she breathes?

"But hand me the phone," I say, in my usual tone of voice, which is low and quiet, but now controlled by a determined effort. "I speak English. I am able to give my own message."

That I dare to speak, to contest what she says sends her into a spasm of wrath. "Why you *black bitch!*" she screams, letting the receiver fall to the level of her own ear and allowing Mrs. Randle, on the other end, to hear her. "You think you can come in here, tell me how to run my business!" Her eyes narrow, like snake eyes, as she orders, "You git out of here!" The small room is a cauldron of hatred, with the New Orleans-bound Greyhound bus driver joining in: "I never seen such an uppity nigger! I know God damn well I'd be man enough to throw her out of here!"

I remain standing, outwardly calm at least, but my insides are churning with fear and anger. I try to remember what I may have said or done to bring on such a volcanic eruption of profanity and why these bitter words are hurled at *me!* Almost paralyzed, I look beyond the woman, to the door with the open-close window, and to the faces of Negro mothers framed inside the window. They are aware of my plight; they have lived through similar debasements all their lives. If they seem unfeeling and unmoved, it is their armor, their protective wall. They can never escape their blackness. "*Black bitch*"—the words ring in my ears, and I try to smile at the two faces framed in the door window, but they simply stare, witnesses to an obscene ritual they take for granted, the hurt and hate stoically suppressed.

"If you don't git out of here *this instant*," the white woman screams, "I'll call the police!"

"Yes," I say, in a voice I hardly know. "You do that."

She dials the police, screams into the instrument, "A Nigra in here causing a disturbance!" In this moment I sit down in the chair in front of her desk, to wait. I don't mind going to jail, but I don't want to go to jail. I will not turn a hand to bring it about, or a hand to prevent it. I look beyond the crazed face of the white woman to the faces of the vulnerable black women, and I think: What if one of them now sat in my shoes? What if one of those women had dared to use this phone?

I hear the white man moving to unlock the main door, and a young black man, neatly dressed and with a self-assured step, walks in.

"What you want, *boy?*" the white owner asks.

"Wait a minute," and the young Negro keeps his ground. "What do you mean by *boy?*"

The white man rephrases his question: "Well, what do you want?"

The young Negro asks about a particular bus, the white owner mutters a time schedule, and the black man leaves.

The scene barely registers on my troubled mind. I soon hear a siren in the distance. Within minutes through the front plate-glass window I see a patrol car pull up to the Dixie Welding Supply–Greyhound Bus station. It's too much for me to comprehend that the commotion and the police concern me. I can't remember my crime.

Oh yes, I remember, and I must keep my wits! I will tell the policeman that I asked to use the telephone, I will be very quiet and *nice* and the policeman will know immediately that I am a respectable, good citizen. But then I know that I am black, and that the policeman likely will believe whatever the white people say against me. He is not really responsible, in a way. He is what he is because of his upbringing, his training, his conditioned reflexes, all of which instruct him to believe the "truth," as the whites say it. I know that I will only prove the point of the whites, that I am an "uppity Nigra" if I try to explain my side of the story.

The siren goes silent and the uniformed cop jumps out of his car, checks his gun, and bounds into the station, his hand on his pistol, "What's the trouble in here!"

"This here uppity Nigra," the white woman screams, "causing a commotion. . . ."

The tall bus driver with the hawk nose: "I know God damn well I'd have thrown her out long before now."

"Thinks she can just take over the place, wouldn't stay over there," says the white owner nodding to his segregated waiting room for Negroes, "where she belongs."

The officer listens to each white person berate me as something akin to a low criminal, and when I attempt to tell him that I merely asked to use a telephone, "and isn't this a bus station, and isn't a bus station supposed to have a public phone?" he does not listen to me, but peremptorily orders me to go to the patrol car outside.

He has me in custody, and clearly plans to take me, as a prisoner, to the Indianola jail when a white priest steps from a car parked a short distance from the police car. I notice that the same young black militant whom the white station owner had called "boy" is with the priest.

"Who are you arresting?" the priest asks.

"She was causing a disturbance, loud talking . . . ," the cop's voice trails off.

"Are you arresting her? Do you have charges?" the priest persists.

"I'm Father Walter," the priest tells me, and the black man adds: "And I'm Rudy Shields." I give my name and they now tell me that Carver Randle has asked them to meet me.

The patrolman now starts to back off like a frightened bully. "Well, well," he says nervously, associating the priest with the power of the Catholic Church and Rudy with the power of the NAACP. "I'll release her, to *your* custody." Then he climbs into his car and speeds off, but this time without his siren on.

Nothing distinguishes Father Walter as an ally of militant blacks. He is so unassuming as to be hard to describe. Of medium height, with glasses, a pleasant manner, soft-spoken, he looks like a priest or a farmer or a small-town businessman. His turned collar identifies him, and for Shields and his people his courage bespeaks all the distinction he needs as a man of the cloth and civil-rights fighter.

When the priest, Shields, and I get into the car, Rudy explains that he walked into the station, came back out, and said to Father Walter, "There's a black woman in there, she seems to be having some problems." He says they waited a few minutes, thinking I might be on a later bus. "Randle had explained that you were a white woman, passing as a Negro, but I didn't expect to see a *real* black woman," Shields says.

"Now I remember your coming in," I say, "but I was so upset, as you can imagine."

"We gotta put a stop to that," Rudy says. "Ninety per cent of the passengers who ride Greyhound in the state of Mississippi are black. We shouldn't have to put up with these conditions. Without the black people they'd go out of existence in this state; same is true with Trailways."

From the bus station, Father Walter and Rudy Shields drive me to the modest frame home of Mrs. Nanie Tubbs, a widow, where I'm to stay while in Indianola. Walking into her warm, commanding presence, I know "the child" will never be too big to go to that mother's arms. A gas stove blazes in her small, comfortable living room with its oversized chairs and sofa. We all proceed at once to the kitchen, however, because Mrs. Tubbs has to cut up chickens and prepare them for the skillet. From her flows the protective spirit of the homemaker, and it washes over Rudy, the priest, and me like a soothing unguent. Her husband of thirty-six years is dead and her ten children are now all grown and living elsewhere, but Mrs. Tubbs remains the mother of a multitude.

A Catholic convert, she attends services at Father Walter's church, St. Benedict the Moor, with a predominately black membership. When she's not there praying she's there helping to plan Negro boycotts of white stores.

"If we can't get to the white people's minds, we'll get to their pocketbooks," Mrs. Tubbs says. "Then maybe they'll listen. The white racists are bad enough, but the Uncle Toms are even worse," she says with quiet emphasis. "In the schools, the black children don't have the classrooms, teachers, books that the white kids have. Two Uncle Tom principals do just what the white folks want them to do; they're supposed to be our 'leaders,' but they're holding us back, holding back the progress of Negro children.

"We tell the white folks: these Uncle Toms have got to go. Fire them, or you're going to have trouble from us. But the whites naturally want to keep them on, to do their bidding. So we calls for a boycott of the downtown stores; all of them are white-owned."

At a St. Benedict the Moor rally the next day Father Walter tells a gathering of black militants: "We have to take a look at the black people who are breaking the boycott. And we have to do something about it. We have to 'educate' the black people to stay away from those white-owned stores.

"And if they don't respond to 'education' I've heard say there is somebody called 'the spirit' that goes around and perhaps 'the spirit' will be able to educate them."

After the meeting, the militants fan out over the downtown areas to "educate" any black shoppers who are breaking the boycott. Among the militants are six teen-age girls, Pearl, Lula Belle, Dorothy Mae, Bessie, Annie Lou, and Willette. They see black women shoppers coming out of a grocery store, and Pearl grabs their cabbages and smashes them over their heads. This, in Father Walter's words, is letting "the spirit" descend.

Sirens sound and the police arrive and cart the spirited girls off to jail.

Later, when Father Walter and Rudy Shields have been able to raise $500 in bail, I go with Rudy Shields to get the girls out of jail.

When we enter, the police chief has big Pearl, only fifteen, and already the mother of a child, out in front of his desk, lecturing her. She looks enormous, dressed in male clothes, with rough Levis, shoes, and a man's shirt hanging outside the pants. The policeman, thin, middle-aged, and very white, upbraids Pearl about her immorality, her illegitimate baby. But the girl stands her ground, sullen, defiant.

"Some of *your* crimes are worse!" she suddenly blurts in his face. "Yes, I know all about my mistake. You don't need to lecture me about that. I know more about it than you do. I show my crime, you don't show yours. They're all buried, you can't see 'em. This is why I'm working in civil rights. And why I'll give my life, too. The ones younger than me, and my baby, are going to have a better chance than I've had."

Her tirade ends when she sees Rudy and me. "Where are the others?" Rudy asks.

"They've got us all locked up. He just brought me out to tell me how bad I am," Pearl says.

"The bail is $500," the officer says, and Rudy takes a wry pleasure in directing the policeman, "Start writing, I have it."

As the girls come out one by one, Lula Belle says, "The police was using profanity language, and then I say, 'You are using profanity language,' and he says, 'What did you say?' And I told him he was using profanity language and he said he wasn't, but everybody in there heard him say it."

"Say what?" I ask.

"Said," she tells me, " 'We're not gonna have this in Indianola, we're tired of yo' damn ass, we'll beat yo' damn ass'—and then the captain, he slung me against the wall. Yes, he did, the captain did," she continues. "And they hit Dorothy Mae, and tried to make her say 'Yes, sir,' and 'No, sir,' and she wouldn't do it, she just laughs in his ole face. Then they lock us up and they say, 'It's gonna be a *long* time before you get out of here!' "

I ask the girls what they did in their cells.

"We sung freedom songs and we sung spirituals," Bessie says. "We sung 'We Shall Overcome' and 'Go Tell It on the Mountain' and 'Free at Last' and 'We Are Soldiers in the Army.' "

Back at Mrs. Tubbs: How close I feel to her, how rare and

wonderful it is when two women have that warm, intimate, confiding kinship. We can talk to each other, freely.

Despite a hard life of work, setbacks, tragedy, her triumphant spirit has sustained her. Her late husband never earned more than forty-two dollars a week and yet they managed to give all ten of their children out-of-state college educations. "They wouldn't have a chance otherwise," she says proudly.

She worked in the fields alongside her husband, and also worked as a maid in white homes. When I relate how the Jackson housewife spoke to me in the most intimate way about her sex life, Mrs. Tubbs shakes her head and says:

"They do that, they do that. Like they tell you they're going out with a man, and I say, 'Don't tell it to me 'cause they say if you eat the *deaf ear*,' and they say, 'What is that?' and I say, 'Thing on a hog's heart, a little flap, on a hog's heart or a cow's, and if you eat that, you tell everything you know; and just like I might tell yo' husband when he come home. Yes, ma'am, I ate that *deaf ear* and I just might tell him.' But they want to talk to you about all that. And they ask you about Negro womens, and if you know if such and such a woman goes with such and such a white man, and mostly I says, 'Really, I don't because I don't be out there.'

"But they treat you, well, you are black, and this is your place, *back here*, but then when trouble comes, you are in the most important place in their lives, they're leanin' on you, in their troubles, whenever they can get some good out of you, they're leanin' on you for it. Even if it's crying on your shoulder.

"They know what trouble is. They know what it is for one of their kids to die. But why kill yours? Why kill the black kid? That's a woman's child. They know how hard it is if one of their kids get out there in an automobile and wreck it and he's dead. But why take night riders and kill the black man? That's somebody's child. But still they cry on your shoulder, always about some little thing they could have avoided had they said, 'This is the way to do things, the human way to do it, not the white way, but the human way.'

"I never had one of my daughters working in a white man's kitchen," Mrs. Tubbs continues. "None of my kids. *Never*. Because I've known a white man to take advantage of the colored woman so much, and every time they take advantage of them they dump it over in the Negro race. I knowed if I keep 'em at home they couldn't get to them so that's what I did, I kept mine at home, all the time. If they wanted to go to the fields and pick some cotton they could do that, if they wanted to hoe some, they could do that, but *not* work in that kitchen, where you come in tangle with that white man, while his wife was out.

"See all the mulattos and you know that happened, because they didn't come from the Negro man with the white woman, it had to come from the white man with a Negro woman. They put it in the trash can because they put it back in the black race, and there's blue eyes and everything, you'll meet 'em, they're Negroes, but they're white still.

"A Negro always is in need for something, as a black person. If you're not pretty schemey, if you don't learn to save your pennies you're always in need for something, and that's where the white man comes in, and get his thing, see. And plenty of 'em go out, y'know, with 'em, and I've knowed 'em to just leave their wives, and go on off with a Negro woman as far as they're concerned. But usually it's the moonlight stuff. Their wives at home and they are moonlighting on the Negro side of town. Well, and a Negro man can't do nothin' about it. Sometimes the Negro man is killed about it. That's the sad picture about it.

"And the white man always handles it so that he looks better than the Negro. He's got the white woman scared to death of the Negro. And every white woman that howls 'Rape,' the

Negro wasn't raping her. Maybe he didn't do the things he wanted to do because he was afraid. And then just happened to look at a white woman, but it wasn't that he tried to rape her.

"If a white girl would come up with a Negro baby, he's not going to be born, they're gonna kill that woman 'fore she has that baby, or get rid of her and that baby both. But the white man he can do it. Sure. You can see it. Some white men have recognized their children, they give 'em a part of their living, but they give it to their Negro children as something special they did for them, not like their own white children, there's a mighty few of 'em do that because they don't wanna."

While we are talking, a neighbor, Mrs. Annie Baker, comes in. She voices the same sentiments:

"I'd never allow one of my daughters to work in a white man's kitchen. You can see, 'monst us, the results, almost white Negroes. Now it's been all this time, our race is ruint! And didn't no Negro man ruin it! As I used to tell Mrs. Tubbs and them, when the civil-rights workers were here, I say, 'If I had twenty women like me and I had my health and strength,' I say, 'We would get something over.' But it so many of us, we don't have the nerve to get up and speak up! Skeered! I'm seventy-four years old now, but I just ain't never been skeered or coward like lots of colored people. I guess I got that nerves from my mother, she was a person wasn't skeered of *nothin'*, she'd call a white man if he'd mess with her as quick as she would a Negro. She'd use her fists, what I mean fizz him!

"Here, the white man calls the black man 'boy' and gets away with it. Sure they call em boys. And they scratch their heads! Instead of standing up there and letting 'em know *I'm a man*, like you.

"Here, women are stronger than men. And everything mostly

done is women. We had just one minister here in town and the Lord took him. He was Reverend Willie Porter.

"I still live in hopes, and pray, pray to live to see that our race will come from one hundred years behind and stand up and be counted.

"And these others are something for the other side. See that's our trouble, our leaders, our ministers, our teachers. They've been saying, 'Be patient, just wait, everything's gonna get better,' but you have to help make it better. You ain't gonna get nothin', sitting down holding your hands. Reverend Porter, he believed in voter registration, civil rights, and everything. Now they arrested a group of 'em here, and they had more than the jail could hold, and they carried 'em over yonder and put them on the county farm, and Reverend Porter was in the jail. Well there was a group from here went over there to Moorehead prison after Reverend Porter, now they wanted to get him off because he was the leading minister. He told them—No, he was gonna stay right there until every man what went there come away. He did, he stayed there until they loosed all of them, and when they got back here to the courthouse, myself and others fixed dinner and fed down here to the Baptist school, what got burned. Reverend Porter stayed right on that truck until the last man's foot hit the ground before he got off. He seed 'em all off, and then he got off. *That was a man leading,* wasn't it!"

Late at night, I am like a little child and climb into Mrs. Tubbs's *big bed* (the mama's bed always seems like the *big* bed), and she gives me an extra pillow and we talk far, far into the night.

She tells of her married life, of her husband ("He'd stand up to a white man same as he would a black one") and their children: "We'd sit around on the floor, playing games, me and my husband was just like two of the kids, we *enjoyed* our children. And I'd always tell them, 'You're jest as good as anybody else, you ain't no better, but you're jest as good,' but my husband, he was so proud of them kids, he said to 'em, 'You are the best, ain't no kids as fine as you.'"

She tells me how they'd struggled, gone without food themselves in order to provide for their children. And how she faced up to Christmas. "I straight away told my kids there weren't no Santa Claus."

"You didn't want to tell them a lie?" I ask.

"No, how could I see my husband working like a slave so we could buy a few oranges, a few toys, and then tell those kids, 'A *white man* brought you these goodies?' No, I say straight away, 'Yo' daddy, ain't no daddy fine as yo' daddy, and *he* brought you these toys!'"

The next evening there's a church supper in the St. Benedict the Moor recreation room, and with two or three exceptions, everyone is black. A white Catholic woman, who has become friendly with Mrs. Tubbs, has brought her white husband for the first time, and he looks embarrassed and ill at ease in this sea of black.

"You want something t'eat?" Mrs. Tubbs asks him.

"I donno," he tells her, completely lost now that his wife has drifted among the Negro women.

"I can fix you somethin' back in the kitchen," Mrs. Tubbs offers.

"Fine, fine," he says.

His wife takes her plate and sits among the Negroes, at long tables. I follow the white man and Mrs. Tubbs into the kitchen, and am fascinated by the sight of the discomfited white man being led away like a child by the large black woman with the expansive personality.

Mrs. Tubbs talks to him in a maternal manner, obviously hoping to put him at ease. He responds and relaxes, and is no longer self-conscious as he digs into the fried chicken and homemade chocolate cake with white icing she places before him.

"Now, what's the difference?" Mrs. Tubbs asks him.

The man drinks some of his punch and says, "That's good, that's really good." With a double take, he asks— "The difference?"

Mrs. Tubbs laughs, and ignores his question. He finishes his meal, and says with genuine relish, "I really enjoyed that, I thank you."

She's serious now. "You are so welcome."

Some of the militant black teen-age girls come into the kitchen to confer with Mrs. Tubbs, among them Pearl. Remembering the next day will be Sunday, I casually inquire if any of the girls will go to church with me. "One of the *white* churches," I stress immediately. Pearl and Lula Belle and Dorothy Mae say they'll go. For all of us it represents a challenge because no white church in Indianola has ever been tarnished or honored, as the case might be, by the presence of a black person.

Rudy Shields comes in the kitchen for more cake, and we inform him of our plan. "Good luck!" he sings out, recalling that when he and other civil-rights workers once attempted to storm the barricades, "The good church members stood at the doors with clubs and bats and kept us out."

Father Walter, when he hears of our plan, is elated. He offers to drive some of us past the main churches on a kind of reconnaissance mission, and we leap at the chance. It's dark and we can't see much except structures that in the night resemble turreted fortresses.

"There's the First Methodist Church," the priest says. "You *might* be able to get in there. I doubt it, but you might. You'd never be able to get in the First Baptist, though. You know, even their national headquarters is segregated into blacks and whites."

Since Pearl is a Baptist and I am a Methodist we joke about whether I will invite her to "my" church or she will invite me to "her" church. We decide to try the Baptists.

Early Sunday Mrs. Tubbs departs for mass at St. Benedict the Moor, leaving me nervously wondering whether the girls will join me, as we've planned. It is raining, dreary, overcast, cold. Finally I telephone the First Methodist and explain I am in town from Jackson. A Berl Adkins, evidently a member in good standing, says "You'll certainly be more than welcome!"

At 11 A.M. Mrs. Tubbs calls. "Aren't they there?"

"No, and it's so late."

She assures me, "The girls will be there; they told you they would. And they'll keep their word."

Hanging up, I find a couple of Mrs. Tubbs's hats, and alternately try one, then the other. One is a floppy black velvet that leaves the worst part of my raven hair showing, while the other is a tall black stovepipe that must make Mrs. Tubbs look formidable indeed. It does nothing for me but make me look ridiculous. I choose the floppy number.

Eleven-twenty. And the girls, Pearl, Willette, and Dorothy Mae arrive. "Are we too late? I think we're too late. Do you still want to try it?" they ask, all at once.

They are extremely nervous. Willette worries about her hem that is coming loose. "No one will notice that!" I assure her, knowing the whites will never take their eyes off her blackness, but I suggest she check Mrs. Tubbs's cluttered dresser for a safety pin, while I phone for a taxi.

Willette and Dorothy Mae and I get in the back of the taxi, all of us stone silent. Big Pearl is up front. I have seen Pearl only in Levis, but now she looks completely different!

Her hair simple and lovely, she is dressed in a way that makes her look half the size she appears in the rough men's attire. We are near the First Baptist Church when Pearl mutters, in a low monotone: "I'd feel better with Bessie being here." Her voice, husky and halting, has a doomlike overtone. I know Pearl means to go back for the stray sheep, Bessie, but the whole plan can now be ruined, for we are already very late. "What do you *all* think?" I ask, resignedly.

No one speaks. It's not my decision. "You decide, Pearl. Whatever you say."

Now Pearl speaks, "I'd feel better with Bessie." She instructs the driver where to go and we wheel away from the church to call for Bessie. When Pearl goes inside, she finds Bessie has already taken off her Sunday clothes, but Lula Belle is there, and dressed adequately, so *she* decides to join us.

Back to the church. It stands like a fortress on a corner. "Where's the main entrance?" I ask the girls, but no one has the faintest notion.

We try a half-dozen doors and finally I open one and peek inside and quickly notice that if we go in there we'll be smack in the midst of it all, far down front and almost in direct line with the pulpit. I can't see any empty pew and I shudderingly conclude that we will have to go in singly and sit among the good brethren and sisters.

"Will you go?" I ask Pearl.

She nods. Pearl and Willette and I walk in, and there on the second row is an empty space next to a man guarding a child stretched out in sleep. He starts to move the child; then horrified he realizes we are *black* people and to discourage and thwart us, he stretches out the child the length of the empty space. Our poise intact, we move ahead and take command of the first row.

Dorothy Mae and Lula Belle are missing, and while I hurry out to find them the choir finishes its final strains of an

eighteenth-century English dirge. As we take our seats the
stone structure of the church seems to tremble with the weight
of our presence. Now all five of us sit, our faces lifted, like
hungry children waiting to be fed.

We have arrived so late that all the preliminaries, all the
singing of hymns by the congregation, the Scripture reading,
the passing of plates for the collection of money to do good
in this world, all of that has ended. Now comes the moment
for the preacher to stand, and he has no choice but to get up
before us all.

What will he say in a time like this? What will he say to
his mixed flock? That we are all God's children? Will he suggest that we all try to forget our pettiness, our cheapness, and
think about things eternal, that God is in his Heaven and all
is right up there but that we have a mess down here on earth?
Or that we are all born and live but for a moment and then
die, and in the meanwhile, isn't love better than *fear?*

The preacher stands. He is tall, over six feet, handsome,
with a new suit, and a carnation placed just right in his lapel.
He rocks slightly on his feet.

"There comes a time," he begins, "in a minister's life when
he just does not know *which way to turn,* just what he should
do." And he is indicating to his flock, nearly jolted out of
their wits, the evil is among them, right down front. You
always have to be on guard against Satan.

"But such a time calls for *calmness* on our part," he says,
determinedly calm. Stay calm, we can pray on Sundays and
lynch on Mondays. His tactic, we figure, is to buck the crisis
back to the congregation, give them time to take the matter
in their own hands if they desire. In effect he is copping out,
pleading, What shall I do? But he plows on, "Under the circumstances, I think we will all stay as calm as possible, and
proceed with the sermon."

It is a catalogue of platitudes. He urges the people to stay firm in their convictions, to stand up for freedom and democracy, and to fight their wars to total victories.

As the excitement of the moment carries him to new heights of passion, he declares with a startling bellow that "I am a Christian!" but to me, he is something less, a slavish captive of his audience (they pay his salary). He is in bondage to them. His belief has not liberated his soul or mind. Like most of the Southern white Christian churches, his is not a Christian church but a social institution, designed to perpetuate the status quo.

A man in the choir rolls his eyes and develops a nervous twitching of his shoulders. Another male choir member rivets a hateful look on Pearl. She leans toward me, proposing in a somewhat too loud voice, "Let's go integrate the First Methodist Church!"

The stares of hatred about us have become so venomous that the poison is stifling and we breathe in short, tentative gasps.

"I want to go," Pearl says. The others quickly agree, and we rise and walk out, briskly but plainly scared.

At the door a man accosts us: "You didn't come here *to worship God!*" he spits his words. "You came here merely to say you'd been in *this church!*"

"Why did you come?" I ask. Stunned, he slams the door behind us.

Outside, one church member dashes from a front door as if bent on violence, but we refuse to bolt. And another from the back door. Neither seems to want to confront us. I advance to where one is standing.

"Did you want to say something?"

"We've called the police. They'll have plenty to say to you all! You'll be locked up, that's what!"

We start walking away. The church is in the center of town, and everywhere the doors are closed. There are no friends to seek out, no telephone booth. And out of nowhere looms the police car, its siren needlessly rupturing the Sunday stillness. It parks across the street from where we are walking, and the cops motion us over.

"Your names, please," asks the police captain, who for some reason appears more nervous than we. He can hardly write, I notice, and he spells my name "Grayce Hall," although I enunciate it with special care.

"You gonna lock us up for going to church?" Pearl asks. She is, as the Southern saying goes, "something else." She is blindly, often imprudently, fearless.

"I don't know what they gonna try to do," the policeman says.

"Who's they?" Pearl persists. The captain says he means the church people. As far as the police are concerned, they will not press charges for "going to church."

They finally allow us to go our way.

"A white man, he can go to any black church, anywhere. No one calls the police," Pearl comments with a lingering bitterness.

Again at Mrs. Tubbs. She's gone to visit a sick neighbor. I listen to the silence, expecting to hear a siren. Are the police on their way to arrest me, goaded by the enraged Baptists? It seems illogical and ridiculous that one can be arrested for going to church, but I know that in Indianola it is possible.

Rudy Shields comes by, and I am glad to see him. He starts talking of some of his experiences, getting me to laugh—and I turn on my tape recorder, taking down verbatim this incident involving preachers:

"Down at Port Gibson, we tried to integrate a white church, but when we got there, they were all standing out there with their bats and clubs. I asked the white minister, did he feel this was right, since we were all worshipping one God, and he told me yeah, he thought it was right because we should worship in the black church. I told him there's only one God, but he told me, 'No, there is a black God for you and a white God for us.' Yeah, he really believes this.

"So, we went around to some of the others, there's more churches on this one street than any other street in Mississippi, about six of 'em. Every church we went to they was lined up across the entrance to block us from coming in and once we marched past without making an attempt to enter and they all turned around and went in, and then we turned and followed 'em in. And we took seats in the rear. Apparently they didn't know we was there for a while and then they discovered we was there. They'd have rather had a killin' than leave us there; they started a fight, y'know, right there in the church. And my buddy Reverend Kilmore was standin' there a-praying and stuff.

"And I said, 'Reverend Kilmore, we got a fight on our hands, whatta you doing, praying?' And he said, 'I'm asking God what should I do,' and I said, 'Well has he told you anything yet?' And he said, 'Yes, he told me to use what I got,' and then he started knockin' hell out of 'em.

"Nonviolence worked for a while, but then we began to realize that this racist in the South, nonviolence just don't work with him. For instance, every county that Reverend Martin Luther King went into there was mass violence, I mean *one-sided* violence where black people was beaten up. Take Charles Evers' movement, for instance. We have boycotted towns and we have really hurt this white racist in Mississippi, but very seldom is there any violence involved because we have this slogan, we live with this slogan: *If you kill my cat I'll get your dog.*

"This the white racist understands. For instance, take St. Benedict the Moor recreation hall; we told 'em if they bomb this center we gonna get some of their buildings, and they understand this, see, and it's the only thing they respect. And this is why I say the nonviolence movement is dead. And then the black man has become more and more radical.

"No, no, it's hard to get him to wait another ten years! He feels his back's up against the wall, that he has nothing to lose; that's the way I feel. I'd just as soon get killed here than go to Vietnam and get killed, for at least I feel that I have a cause here. If you ask a man to lay down his life you gotta have a cause. And I think a person under thirty-five, he doesn't care anything about life because we're not living, we're just existing and so we get it any way we can and we do.

"There are very few black people in the state of Mississippi that's not armed—shotgun, rifle, or something.

"I've been in some peoples' homes who had high-powered rifles in every corner and Charles Evers has guards around his home, and I have to guard mine every night. But we've found that as long as they know you're pulling guard, that you will protect your property, you don't have too much trouble out of 'em. The Klan as a whole, they're a bunch of cowards, that's why they ride around at night with a hood over their head; they're scared, they'll never attack you unless they got you outnumbered or the odds are heavy in their favor. On Election Day, 1968, this white fellow thought he'd finally caught me by myself and he took out his gun and threatened to shoot me, but I was quick to show him I had a gun, too. Then he suddenly did a disappearing act.

"To some people who are outside the state our carrying guns sounds very radical, but it's just a matter of survival if you want to live in Mississippi. The *only* way to survive is to let the white people know that we will defend ourselves. We don't look for trouble, but if he starts killing we're gonna have to get some of his people.

"I'll say this, being in Mississippi the last few years, I believe that Mississippi will solve this racial problem quicker than most of your Northern states. By '76 black people will be in control of the whole state of Mississippi. And I think we're going to solve the race problem. And this racist down here, in spite of the fact that he'll blow your brains out, in his mind he's a good Christian. And black people and white people live close together and there's more communication between the two races of people in Mississippi than what it'd be in Chicago, or any big city like that, where the blacks and whites are completely separate.

"Here, white and black live together. Well, a block from where I live I have a white neighbor. Of course, you wouldn't never know, I never see her, but that's just how close we live down here together. And as far as the white man goes, as long as you stay 'in your place' he'll do you a favor.

"I found this, for instance in Chicago, I was very involved in civil rights and the place where I was employed many of the white people that worked there would ask me, 'Why do the Negroes demonstrate?' and 'Why do you march and do things like that?' And I'd tell them about some of the conditions, not only in Mississippi but right there in Chicago, practically on their doorsteps, and you know, they wouldn't believe me! I remember once I took a couple of white fellows over into the black ghettos. I took them into some of the rat-infested buildings and showed them how black people lived, and they all said, 'If I were black, if I had to live under these circumstances, I'd be demonstrating, too.' But in Chicago I saw there was just no communication between black and white."

From Indianola, I take a bus to Clarksdale. I will stay in the home of a Negro woman, Vera Pigee, who will be out of town. Alex Waites had telephoned Vera Pigee from Jackson about me and immediately she offered her key. "I trust her if you trust her," she told Alex. And that's the way it is with the freedom fighters of Mississippi, they trust one another as soul brothers and soul sisters, simply without explanations or reservations. Theirs is a bond forged in tribal griefs and tempered by the act of survival.

In Clarksdale, I take a taxi, and am introduced to "niggertown" in familiar fashion: it is where the paved streets end and the muddy ones begin. Negroes all through Mississippi make bitter jokes about how whitey builds paved roads *around*, never through, their communities. Vera's house on Baird Street has a front yard no bigger than a child's sandy playpen, with a little knee-high white picket fence. Vera has left the key in the mailbox by prearrangement with Alex and I open the door into a small living room; a long hallway leads off it to the kitchen and a bedroom. As I relax on the edge of the bed, I hear the rain and the ominous howling of Vera's police dog, which is kept in a small enclosure in the back of the house. Night riders have fired into her home, and the bullet hole in the front door is a gaping reminder that terror is a companion of every black man and woman in Clarksdale.

If any Klansmen discover that I am white and being sheltered in this Negro home, they may try to bomb the place. The awareness of this threat, coupled with the loneliness, the cold, damp isolation of my existence, well up in me, and being unable to combat it, I find an oddly perverse pleasure in it, drawing it closer, as an old woman huddles in her shawl. Vera's things, her clothing, record player, souvenirs of her happy times, only accentuate the strangeness I feel at being black in a black woman's home. I am worse than lonely. I feel disembodied, a cipher floating in a void, for without black people surrounding me, I do not feel a Negro; yet in surroundings that are Vera's I cannot be my old self, either.

In a deep funk, I trudge off to the State Employment office and now rather adept at writing with my left hand, fill out a work application card. A woman, fluttery, feminine, with beautiful long tapering fingers, invites me to sit at her desk while she goes over my history. "And how long did you work at Harlem Hospital?" She flips her hands upward, admiring her nails, while I contemplate her question. "How long?" And how does one measure it, in statistical or psychic terms? In days, weeks, months, or by the scars of experience? By the reality of the calendar or the reality of what it had *seemed*, say, at least two years? I say something inane and vague about it seeming like years, and she laughs, approvingly.

"That's good, Grace, *good*." I suppress the urge to snap back, "There was nothing *good* about it."

Posters proclaiming "WANTED: fruit pickers," and urging Mississippi laborers to go to Florida, are plastered on the walls of the office. It's all part of the racists' scheme, I muse. Failing in their last-ditch attempts to keep "the nigger" in his place, the white Mississippians now are encouraging, even forcing, an exodus of Negroes to other states.

My reverie is shattered by the woman's voice: "Would you like a job washing dishes?" She holds a card in her hand.

"Yes," I say, "I'll take anything."

"It pays three dollars a day, but Mr. Marvin at Rancheros will want to interview you first," she says. Every maid, every factory worker, every dishwasher with whom I talk say they are grilled regularly about their political, religious, and social beliefs and activities, and I suspect Mr. Marvin will subject me to a similar catechism.

With no local bus service in Clarksdale, I'm obliged to call a taxi to go to my interview as a dishwasher.

Rancheros is a small eatery, part drive-in and part indoor restaurant, out on Highway 61. It is still raining when I arrive and approach Mr. Marvin, who is standing at the cash register.

"Yeah, I can sure use you," he says, without preliminaries. "Will you be here at ten?" I nod. "Well, we open right at ten, so you come at that time."

The next morning I again hire a taxi but this time a different Mr. Marvin is at the cash stand. "No," he growls, "I ain't got no job. I don't need you, and I don't know why my brother told you to come." I stare at him, speechless.

"You heard me! Now git out of here!"

Out in the rain again. He's made no offer to pay for the taxis I have used for two days, or to apologize for the time and inconvenience he and his brother have caused. Instead he has taken the position that it had been my fault that his brother hired me.

The taxi that picks me up going back to town has another passenger, a Negro woman who tells me she works as a maid from 7 A.M. to 6 P.M., and makes fifteen dollars a week.

The white driver interjects the remark that "Lots of times the white folks here pay the maids' taxi fares," and I laugh contemptuously, thinking he's made an ironic joke, but seeing his face in the rear-view mirror, I realize he thinks it's Southern kindness to pay a woman three dollars *and fifty cents* (the fifty cents for a cab) for a ten- or eleven-hour day of menial labor.

Another day and I am back at the State Employment Office, where another clerk produces the name of a white family, Wheeler, that wants someone for housecleaning and ironing. I agree to take the job, and Mrs. Wheeler, who works in her family's supply store, drives by to pick me up. Her husband, I learn, is an official in the Clarksdale bank, whose president heads the White Citizens Council, a sort of housebroken or urbanized Ku Klux Klan.

Mrs. Wheeler, already dressed for work at the office, remains at home only long enough to outline my chores, which by now are falling into a repetitive pattern (clean the commode, clean the tub, clean the floors, run the sweeper, do the washing, do the ironing), and then she departs in her Impala.

Melissa, a teen-age daughter, whose bedroom is a shambles, panties left where she's stepped out of them, bra on the floor nearby, slip there, shoes here, empty Cokes amid an assortment of dolls, breezes in and out. "Are you going to be permanent?" she asks, not waiting for an answer. Eventually, she drives off in what is apparently her own car. The comings and goings of the family members give the house an air of impermanence, with the kind of emotional kinship and stability you'll find in a hotel lobby.

The two-story colonial home is probably in the $50,000 bracket, with master bedroom, Melissa's bedroom, a bedroom-bath suite for Mr. Wheeler's blind mother (now away in some hospital) and a large den, as well as two other baths, large kitchen, dining room, and living room. Cleaning Melissa's room, making her bed, picking up all of her scattered clothing and seeing how little regard she has for her expensive dresses, I wonder how any "young" man can ever make enough money to support her. And if she marries a Northerner, she'll have to learn to hang up her own clothes and look after herself. She might even have to adopt the philosophy I heard from a black mother, a widow with seven children: "You jest manages, when you gotta."

I run the sweeper in all the bedrooms, sweep the kitchen, dust all the furniture, and am in the midst of bringing in the sheets from the clothesline (Southerners still "sun" their clothes rather than dry them in machines) when I notice that a car different from Melissa's or Mrs. Wheeler's is pulling into the drive and I presume the current "visitor" to be Mr. Wheeler.

I fold the sheets and pillowcases and sprinkle them for ironing. Mr. Wheeler, in his late forties, with a receding hairline, medium build, with soft body muscles that come from too much sitting, enters the kitchen. I do not look at him directly but keep my eyes to the laundry, yet I sense he is staring at me, and in that moment of silence, I feel he is somehow magnetized.

He speaks in a businesslike manner, almost as if he is appraising a piece of jewelry. At the same time there is a proprietary familiarity about his manner, as if I might be a newly acquired piece of furniture. He asks the usual: what's my name and how long have I been in Clarksdale, but as we talk I know he's incapable of seeing what I represent for myself alone.

He leaves the room after a time. Soon from his mother's suite comes a thunderous clap (the blind woman's fish bowl has fallen from its stand is my first reaction) and simultaneously he shouts, "Come quick!"

Hurrying upstairs, I walk swiftly into the bedroom. Instantly the door slams behind me and as I turn around I find myself encircled in Wheeler's arms. I am momentarily overwhelmed. He presses his mouth roughly against mine and forces his body against me, muttering hoarsely about his desperate need for "black pussy." He has already unzipped his trousers, indicating he intends few if any preliminaries. His muscles strain against me and he uses his arms like a vise to keep me from breaking away and at the same time force me onto the bed.

"Only take five minutes, only take *five minutes*," he mumbles, partly pleading, partly threatening. "Now quieten down! Just gotta get me some black pussy!"

I try frantically to break his hold but he has my arms pinioned, and we fall awkwardly onto the bed near the headboard. Then he crawls on top of me. I feel myself suffocating from his body weight and panting breath. I wriggle free after some effort and start to run but he jumps after me and pins me against a wall, pushing me practically through the woodwork. I realize he is holding me under a huge and ghastly oil painting of the entire family, in an ornate frame that must weigh a ton. I loose one arm enough to reach up and, with the last of my strength and willpower, I push the large framed picture from its moorings and send it careening down. It grazes the back of Wheeler's head.

His flushed face dissolves from lust into hatred. "You black bitch!" he cries, shaking with anger. More menacingly he adds, his voice lowered to a whisper: "I ought to kill you, you black bitch!"

I suppose I should feel terror-stricken all over again; the lord and master is in a state of mind where nothing might faze him, and where the urge to satisfy himself as a punitive act may be strong. But curiously my feeling is one of utter relief. Then, feeling more contempt than fear: "Go ahead, you coward!" I dare him. "You wouldn't have the nerve!"

He is spared from accepting this challenge by the striking of the grandfather clock in the bedroom. It reminds him apparently that his wife and daughter are due home soon and that unless he has time to rehang the picture some explaining will be in order. I imagine he also wants me out of sight before I might be tempted to excite the curiosity of his womenfolk.

I wait for no invitation to leave, however. Dashing downstairs, I fling on my coat and stride out of the house as fast as I can and maintain the pace for several blocks, unable to think straight. When a police car cruises by, I pretend I know where I am going in order to keep from attracting attention. For I now have a fresh worry: has Wheeler called the cops to get his revenge? Would he charge me with having stolen personal property? Have me locked up? Would they even let me use a telephone? Sometimes, I've heard, they don't allow even that in Mississippi. At an intersection I spot a rattling 1960 sedan carrying a group of Negroes. Running up, I blurt out, "I've had an emergency," and ask them if they will drive me into town. They are headed in that direction, and the family, a father, mother and three young children, make room for me, asking no questions.

Surrounded by blackness I now breathe freely, certain that I am in the embrace of those who will protect me, in their understanding of my blackness. Their sympathy makes Wheeler's whitey world bearable for the moment, and while they don't know what has happened, their instincts tell them enough.

We Negroes, I think, cannot love each other, cannot treat each other with such recognition of soul, cannot be so tender, so kind, one with the other, if the whites had not united us, given us our identity by their hatred. The irony of my plight is inescapable and sad: I have desperately fled from the "protection" of the white police, and run back to what now seems the safe shore, the Negro community.

Back at Vera's house I heat a pan of water to bathe my body. How many Negro women, I wonder, have worked all day for white people and never been paid for their labor, never been paid except as I was paid, by an insult, a threat to kill for not bowing before a white man's desire? He could have called the police and then what recourse would the average black woman have if it came down to a question of her word against his? ("Nigger, you know you stole that diamond ring!")

And why, my thoughts race on, could he have been so certain that five minutes of lust for forbidden fruit would be his only for the taking? Not for the asking, but only for the taking? In what depths of contempt he must hold all black women.

I have heard many Negro maids say that their greatest fear is being in the house alone when the white man comes in. As one bitterly commented, "They pay you fifteen dollars a week, and then expect to get you too." I wonder if the proud Southern wife really knows how the family gets its money's worth out of their own "minimum wage."

Traditionally, if the Negro woman wants to keep a job, she all too frequently has to submit to the white man's desires. This has been so commonplace that many Negro mothers say their greatest ambition is to give their daughters enough education so that they'll never have to work in "whitey's kitchen." The words of Mrs. Annie Baker echo in my ear: "Our race has been ruint, and ain't no black man that ruint it." The white man casually rapes the black women, taking them as they would their smokes or bourbon—out of their own greed, their own lusting after the flesh they tell their own women is a dirty, filthy color. And for this reason one sees very few really pure *black* people left in the South. If the Negro husband complains when a man rapes his wife, he is, in the judgment of many Southern whites, getting "uppity" and he risks violence and even death. So the Negro man has never been able to raise his voice.

If I had been a black married woman, could I have told my Negro husband: "Wheeler tried to rape me?" Then what? What could one black man have done against the entire System? Would one black man have the nerve to take a gun and shoot the white man?

On the other hand, I don't think that Wheeler would or could have "made love" with Mrs. Wheeler the way he so desperately desired it with a black woman. He is a proper man (upright member of the community, White Citizens Council member, bank director, deacon in the First Baptist Church), and would make love with his wife in a "proper" way. But my blackness makes a difference.

I, as a white woman, have never seen eyes so full of lust and greed as I have as a black woman looking into the faces of white men who want to possess me. At café cash stands and bus-ticket counters, white men have winked at me, not flirtatiously (as might have happened, had I been white) but in a blatantly open, "come on" way, hinting at a common complicity in violating society's color taboos.

Always, as a black woman among white men, I have felt they considered me as in-season game, easily bagged, no license needed. In downtown New York before the trip South I rode in a taxi with a white friend. At our destination, when my friend handed over the fare, the white driver turned to him, grinned widely, and commented, "You're lucky, my friend. Got yourself a cute little colored hooker!" The white cabdriver had not seen a woman or even a human being, but simply a commodity.

Later, I walked alone from a mid-Manhattan office building. A short, pale-white, middle-aged man approached me, his face an El Greco of agonized desire. Was the man ill? I had not ever seen a face reflecting such ambivalence.

"I will buy you a beer," he said. His hunger, his lust, was almost a visible thing in the crowd. My reluctance caused him to ante his offer: "Or," he added, "a Scotch!"

"No, no, no!" I told him and walked away, but he followed me two, three, four, five blocks.

"If you are busy now," he implored, "I will come to Harlem later."

"No, no!" He was seeing me as I had never seen myself! Always before, impervious, regal, white, I had fanned away unwanted would-be white suitors. But now my status as white, my membership in the club, my pedestal, was missing. He saw me as defenseless. He knew I would not, could not, approach a policeman and complain, "This white man is bothering me." Who would believe that any white American was molesting a colored woman? "*I will make it right to you*," he promised.

What have I done, I wondered, to be turned into a street-walker? His approach, his sticking to me as close as flypaper, his whispering as if he and I were together in some sinful plot left me trembling. I was crushed to the level of the existence I had in his eyes. A few moments before, I might have shouted at him and aroused the attention of those men and women milling in front and back and around us. But now I felt as he had known I would: humiliated, shamed, reduced to mutterings and whispers. I tried to summon vehemence: "I have a husband!" I warned (having given up threatening him with the cops). "He is waiting for me right now."

The white man smiled as if I were but coyly setting the preliminaries for our encounter. Husband? How could he be frightened by a black husband? He bought and sold his kind, hired 'em for peanuts; they didn't make much fuss or bother, they could not. "Oh," he smiled again, indicating *we* have our secrets, we know what we have to do in this world to get bread, pay the rent. And then he told me, "But he's not around all the time," and the words suggested I had only to name the time and place.

To end this absurd encounter as quickly as possible, I darted out into the heavy traffic, then escaped into a subway entrance. That incident was over, finished, that was back in New York, in another place, another time, and I am now safe, safe in Vera Pigee's bed. But where is the balm of sleep? Not sleep, but the memory of Wheeler's face grips and holds me. He has accepted sex as "bad," only to be practiced in the nicest way with his pure white wife. And to be practiced in the "foulest" of ways with black women ("only take five minutes!"), and then like a harassed dog, as a black friend put it, he'd "cover his shit and run." Run? Off to the White Citizens Council to lay the strategy to keep them niggers in their place! He would act no doubt not only out of his hatred for the color of black, but out of his hatred for himself, having *used* it.

I begin to see the role of the black woman in Wheeler's home objectively. She is me, and she is not me, because I could escape. But suppose the black woman in his frenzied embrace had been a mother of hungry children, waiting for her to bring them food. Could she have resisted his advances? Run from the home without collecting *any* money for her day's labor? And suppose Wheeler had won his claim. As he'd insisted, "only take five minutes . . . only five minutes," but what might those five minutes have meant to an overburdened mother?

Suppose he had made the black woman pregnant. The child would be *her* child, not his! For his five minutes of sensuality she would pay for the rest of her life. The child, no matter how "fair" its skin, would be classified as a nigger. The mother would be struggling for food and to pay the rent, sacrificing to give the child even a second-rate education. And Wheeler? He'd be at the bank appraising loans, in the church passing the collection plate, in the White Citizens Council making reports on the crime and violence, and blaming it on the uppity niggers.

At home with Mrs. Wheeler he could listen as she related her frustrations with the Negro maid. She might tell her husband again about the immorality of the blacks, how the black men don't marry black women (but just "live together"), and how they have all those dozens of kids, "breeding 'em like animals."

Now I reflect how I had gone with trembling heart to the ghetto, Harlem, fearful that a big black bogeyman might tear down the paper-thin door separating my "white" body from his lustful desires. And now it had been a white, not a black, devil whose passions had overwhelmed him. His uncontrollable desire for blackness (strange, mysterious, evil—therefore, *good*) simply underscores white Americans' hypocrisy. Sex is what's important, it's the root of all our racial frustrations (and a few more besides!), and the basis for three centuries of lies. The white man created the taboos about blackness and then fell prey to them, desiring the flesh not in spite of but *because* it is black.

Looking back at the centuries-old bedroom scene, seeing Mr. Wheeler with his agonized, bitter hatred of me, and of himself, I realize how sad it is that you and I so often express our real selves not by joy or blissful rapture, but by the kick in the guts we give one another. The problem is larger than black and white. It is man's inhumanity to man (and woman), always and everywhere.

Epilogue

BACK IN JANUARY, 1968, when I told a black Washington law-yer that I planned to disguise myself as a Negro woman and go to the South, he warned, "You will go down there *and get yourself killed.*"

Getting killed is a remote abstraction to me and has never frightened me, anyhow. I turned aside his warning with some flippancy, such as, oh, well, one has to die sometime. Then he made a prediction which had a greater impact: "You will learn to hate your own people."

I dismissed that possibility, at the time, but had reason to remember it time and again in the months that followed.

I chose to begin my venture in Harlem, because of amor-phous fears about the black devil. The ghetto would supply me with a quick and difficult baptism into the life and times of a black woman in this free and heralded society. The hard-ships, the physical discomforts, the controlled fears could be endured best at the outset. After that I could "go home" to the South, to my kind of people, where I could relinquish my fears, heal any lingering wounds in a familiar environment, among the generous and hospitable white Southerners with whom I grew up, whose attitudes and social outlook I shared, in a congenital sense.

My past experiences, living in remote areas, sometimes a thousand miles removed from the nearest doctor or telephone, armed me, after a fashion, for the ghetto. The difficulties of daily living in Harlem or Manaus can be roughly comparable. But I was not prepared for the isolation, the separateness, of Harlem. Let no one think *apartheid* is a South African monopoly; legally, yes, but socially, spiritually, psychologically, no. The Berlin Wall is *papier mâché* compared to the barriers surrounding Harlem. But as a black woman, I found the devils of Harlem less menacing, craven, dishonest, cruel, ruthless, than the "superior" Caucasians of the South. The black devils of Harlem did not attempt to assault me and made no claims that compromised their dignity or mine. I hold no brief for their weaknesses and justify none of their delinquencies. I met them on their terms, as men and women whose color in no way deprived them of the complexes, hopes, fears, strivings, of the desire to make something of value and perhaps beauty out of the squalid and limited alternatives bequeathed them by white America.

Then I went South and was reminded again that nature is no match for man in his wayward ability to inflict pain. Nature can kill and maim, but lacks the capacity for psychic malice, for scarring the mind and spirit, that humans have.

Nothing in all my travels over the past two decades, nothing in my experiences, prepared me for going to the South as a black woman. The emotions I harbored belonged to two persons: a black woman and a white woman. I was cast in a twin, paradoxical role of oppressor and oppressed. I was a vessel of sorts for two personalities, two sets of eyes, two bodies. But the heaviest, and the most unhappy, element in this strange container was a single human heart in conflict with itself. I never resolved the contradictions of the life I undertook to live. That was not my purpose. I wanted only to open my mind, my eyes, my pores, to the dilemma of race in America, and to share those experiences without making claims to the discovery of fresh truths about ourselves. I searched for light and understanding, in the knowledge that any other terrain was unimportant.

Now that it's over I ask myself these questions: Could you do it again? The answer is no. Are you glad that you did it? The answer is yes. And why glad? Because I live in a bigger world and I am black as well as white. I like Gandhi's having said that a part of him was Jew, a part Buddhist, a part Christian.

And why do I say I couldn't do it again? Because now I know what it cost me, psychologically, to bear, for one minute in time, what every black American bears all his life: discrimination, segregation, injustice. I truly journeyed into areas of *apartheid.* Yet by examining the human heart with a kind of stethoscope, one concludes that all classes, groups, and individuals are set apart from each other, the husband from his wife, the child from his mother. We are in one sense self-segregated. It is this isolation from man's inner world—the source of personality, character, and if you like, soul—that pains and cripples the white American, I believe, even more than the black American. Many white Americans have become so estranged from the inner world they argue it does not exist, and even if it does, that it does not matter.

Now the Negroes are shouting at the top of their lungs, "Don't forget soul," reminding us of the emptiness of life without it. White Americans, obsessed by their material goals, driven to protect their gains and gadgets, could learn from the blacks that all the money in the world and what it buys will not bring them "soul."

Someone has asked, "When did you first become interested in the Negroes?"

My travels showed me how the colonial British lived on the laboring masses in India and Malaysia and Hong Kong; and how the colonial French lorded it over the Algerians and how the Spaniards and before them the Incas used slaves to enable a handful of masters to live like monarchs. Finally, I perceived that the "supremacy" of minds, white or black or Inca, is a myth perpetuated to rationalize the master-slave relationship. But that epoch of human degradation is ending. The slaves have found voices and are saying simply, enough, enough.

Between the two, Harlem and the South, the South was more difficult for me. But I ask myself: if you were born black, where would you choose to live, Harlem or the South? And my answer is the South.

In the ghetto one feels he's in a trap, that there is no hope. He fights against an "enemy" that is unseen, and he calls it the System, the Establishment.

In the South it's more a man-to-man conflict. One knows "the man," the enemy. He knows the Klansman, the racist, the oppressor, the murderer by name. But the Negro also knows that a man can change, that attitudes are adaptable. And so in Mississippi the Negroes do have hope. And Southern Negro leaders, such as Charles Evers and Aaron Henry, believe that Southerners, black and white, will solve their problems sooner than the Northern city and suburban dwellers.

Sitting in the Indianola First Baptist Church with the young black militant girls I realized their mission, their message. They were thinking beyond integration to transformation. I thought Pearl could have given a memorable sermon in her passionate, blurting way. I believe she would have told the "Christians" that prayer means sharing their food and changing the conditions of misery for other human beings, not just reciting words asking a Magician-Deity to do it, hoping thereby to absolve the conscience.

Yes, I can see the white people as "my" people, but the Washington lawyer was wrong. I can hate them only if I hate myself. At one time I thought "my people" were Koreans, another time Mexicans, and still another, Peruvians. I cannot escape the fact that I was born a Southern white. But nothing prevents me from feeling spiritually black—or brown, or yellow or red, for that matter. "My people" abide in my heart and mind—and that is the reality that all people must come to know and recognize.

The temptation to preach is overwhelming, but how else does one proclaim the balm of love and the healing quality of understanding?

What did I learn? I learned only what we always forget: that there is no certitude, that we "know" little beyond the fact that life is pain and life is a burden, and often insupportable for those who believe they can walk or live alone.

OTHER BOOKS BY GRACE HALSELL

Peru
Evers: A Biography of Charles Evers
Black-White Sex
Bessie Yellowhair
Los Viejos
The Illegals
Journey to Jerusalem
Prophecy and Politics
In Their Shoes
Forcing God's Hand